A Tale of Two Cities

雙城記

商務印書館

This Chinese edition of *A Tale of Two Cities* has been published with the written permission of Black Cat Publishing.

The copyright of this Chinese edition is owned by The Commercial Press (H.K.) Ltd.

Name of Book: A Tale of Two Cities
Author: Charles Dickens
Text adaptation and notes: James Butler
Activities: Kenneth Brodey
Editors: Rebecca Raynes, Monika Marszewska
Design and art direction: Nadia Maestri
Computer graphics realisation: Sara Blasigh
Illustrations: Anna and Elena Balbusso
Edition: ©2002 Black Cat Publishing
　　　　 an imprint of Cideb Editrice, Genoa, Canterbury

系 列 名：Black Cat 優質英語階梯閱讀 · Level 6
書 　 名：雙城記
責任編輯：黃淑嫺
封面設計：張　毅　曹　磊
出　　版：商務印書館（香港）有限公司
　　　　　香港筲箕灣耀興道 3 號東滙廣場 8 樓
　　　　　http://www.commercialpress.com.hk
發　　行：香港聯合書刊物流有限公司
　　　　　香港新界大埔汀麗路 36 號中華商務印刷大廈 3 字樓
印　　刷：中華商務彩色印刷有限公司
　　　　　香港新界大埔汀麗路 36 號中華商務印刷大廈
版　　次：2013 年 5 月第 1 版第 3 次印刷
　　　　　© 商務印書館（香港）有限公司
　　　　　ISBN 978 962 07 1671 3
　　　　　Printed in Hong Kong

出版説明

　　本館一向倡導優質閱讀，近年來連續推出了以 "Q" 為標識的 "Quality English Learning 優質英語學習" 系列，其中《讀名著學英語》叢書，更是香港書展入選好書，讀者反響令人鼓舞。推動社會閱讀風氣，推動英語經典閱讀，藉閱讀拓廣世界視野，提高英語水平，已經成為一種潮流。

　　然良好閱讀習慣的養成非一日之功，大多數初、中級程度的讀者，常視直接閱讀厚重的原著為畏途。如何給年輕的讀者提供切實的指引和幫助，如何既提供優質的學習素材，又提供名師的教學方法，是當下社會關注的重要問題。針對這種情況，本館特別延請香港名校名師，根據多年豐富的教學經驗，精選海外適合初、中級英語程度讀者的優質經典讀物，有系統地出版了這套叢書，名為《Black Cat 優質英語階梯閱讀》。

　　《Black Cat 優質英語階梯閱讀》體現了香港名校名師堅持經典學習的教學理念，以及多年行之有效的學習方法。既有經過改寫和縮寫的經典名著，又有富創意的現代作品；既有精心設計的聽、説、讀、寫綜合練習，又有豐富的歷史文化知識；既有彩色插圖、繪圖和照片，又有英美專業演員朗讀作品的 CD。適合口味不同的讀者享受閱讀之樂，欣賞經典之美。

　　《Black Cat 優質英語階梯閱讀》由淺入深，逐階提升，好像參與一個尋寶遊戲，入門並不難，但要真正尋得寶藏，需要投入，更需要堅持。只有置身其中的人，才能體味純正英語的魅力，領略得到真寶的快樂。當英語閱讀成為自己生活的一部分，英語水平的提高自然水到渠成。

商務印書館 (香港) 有限公司

編輯部

使用説明 _____

1 應該怎樣選書？

按閱讀興趣選書

《Black Cat 優質英語階梯閱讀》精選世界經典作品，也包括富於創意的現代作品；既有膾炙人口的小説、戲劇，又有非小説類的文化知識讀物，品種豐富，內容多樣，適合口味不同的讀者挑選自己感興趣的書，享受閱讀的樂趣。

按英語程度選書

《Black Cat 優質英語階梯閱讀》現設 Level 1 至 Level 6，由淺入深，涵蓋初、中級英語程度。讀物分級採用了國際上通用的劃分標準，主要以詞彙（vocabulary）和結構（structures）劃分。

Level 1 至 Level 3 出現的詞彙較淺顯，相對深的核心詞彙均配上中文解釋，節省讀者查找詞典的時間，以專心理解正文內容。在註釋的幫助下，讀者若能流暢地閱讀正文內容，就不用擔心這一本書程度過深。

Level 1 至 Level 3 出現的動詞時態形式和句子結構比較簡單。動詞時態形式以現在時（present simple）、現在時進行式（present continuous）、過去時（past simple）為主，句子結構大部分是簡單句（simple sentences）。此外，還包括比較級和最高級（comparative and superlative forms）、可數和不可數名詞（countable and uncountable nouns）以及冠詞（articles）等語法知識點。

Level 4 至 Level 6 出現的動詞時態形式，以現在完成時（present perfect）、現在完成時進行式（present perfect continuous）、過去完成時（past perfect continuous）為主，句子結構大部分是複合句（compound sentences）、條件從句（1st and 2nd conditional sentences）等。此外，還包括情態動詞（modal verbs）、被動形式（passive forms）、動名詞（gerunds）、

短語動詞（phrasal verbs）等語法知識點。

　　根據上述的語法範圍，讀者可按自己實際的英語水平，如詞彙量、語法知識、理解能力、閱讀能力等自主選擇，不再受制於學校年級劃分或學歷高低的約束，完全根據個人需要選擇合適的讀物。

② 怎樣提高閱讀效果？

　　閱讀的方法主要有兩種：一是泛讀，二是精讀。兩者各有功能，適當地結合使用，相輔相成，有事半功倍之效。

　　泛讀，指閱讀大量適合自己程度（可稍淺，但不能過深）、不同內容、風格、體裁的讀物，但求明白內容大意，不用花費太多時間鑽研細節，主要作用是多接觸英語，減輕對它的生疏感，鞏固以前所學過的英語，讓腦子在潛意識中吸收詞彙用法、語法結構等。

　　精讀，指小心認真地閱讀內容精彩、組織有條理、遣詞造句又正確的作品，着重點在於理解"準確"及"深入"，欣賞其精彩獨到之處。精讀時，可充分利用書中精心設計的練習，學習掌握有用的英語詞彙和語法知識。精讀後，可再花十分鐘朗讀其中一小段有趣的文字，邊唸邊細心領會文字的結構和意思。

　　《Black Cat 優質英語階梯閱讀》中的作品均值得精讀，如時間有限，不妨嘗試每兩個星期泛讀一本，輔以每星期挑選書中一章精彩的文字精讀。要學好英語，持之以恆地泛讀和精讀英文是最有效的方法。

③ 本系列的練習與測試有何功能？

　　《Black Cat 優質英語階梯閱讀》特別注重練習的設計，為讀者考慮周到，切合實用需求，學習功能強。每章後均配有訓練聽、說、讀、寫四項技能的練習，分量、難度恰到好處。

聽力練習分兩類，一是重聽故事回答問題，二是聆聽主角對話、書信朗讀、或模擬記者訪問後寫出答案，旨在以生活化的練習形式逐步提高聽力。每本書均配有 CD 提供作品朗讀，朗讀者都是專業演員，英國作品由英國演員錄音，美國作品由美國演員錄音，務求增加聆聽的真實感和感染力。多聆聽英式和美式英語兩種發音，可讓讀者熟悉二者的差異，逐漸培養分辨英美發音的能力，提高聆聽理解的準確度。此外，模仿錄音朗讀故事或模仿主人翁在戲劇中的對白，都是訓練口語能力的好方法。

閱讀理解練習形式多樣化，有縱橫字謎、配對、填空、字句重組等等，注重訓練讀者的理解、推敲和聯想等多種閱讀技能。

寫作練習尤具新意，教讀者使用網式圖示（spidergrams）記錄重點，採用問答、書信、電報、記者採訪等多樣化形式，鼓勵讀者動手寫作。

書後更設有升級測試（Exit Test）及答案，供讀者檢查學習效果。充分利用書中的練習和測試，可全面提升聽、説、讀、寫四項技能。

❹ 本系列還能提供甚麼幫助？

《Black Cat 優質英語階梯閱讀》提倡豐富多元的現代閱讀，巧用書中提供的資訊，有助於提升英語理解力，擴闊視野。

每本書都設有專章介紹相關的歷史文化知識，經典名著更有作者生平、社會背景等資訊。書內富有表現力的彩色插圖、繪圖和照片，使閱讀充滿趣味，部分加上如何解讀古典名畫的指導，增長見識。有的書還提供一些與主題相關的網址，比如關於不同國家的節慶源流的網址，讓讀者多利用網上資源增進知識。

CONTENTS

FCE : First Certificate in English Examination-Style Exercises.

All the chapters are recorded except for Chapters Four, Eight and Ten. 故事選錄

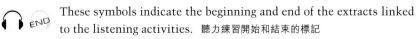

These symbols indicate the beginning and end of the extracts linked to the listening activities. 聽力練習開始和結束的標記

E-1 **E-1** END These symbols indicate the beginning and end of the extracts linked to the listening activities of the **FCE-style exam.**

Charles Dickens

Charles Dickens (1839) by Daniel Maclise (1806-70).
By courtesy of National Portrait Gallery, London.

Charles Dickens, (1812-70), was born in Portsmouth, where his father worked in the Navy pay office. When his father was imprisoned for debt in the Marshalsea prison, the twelve-year-old Dickens was forced to take a job in a factory, a humiliating [1] experience that he would never forget. Many of his novels deal with the theme of poor or abandoned children.

After working as a shorthand [2] reporter in the House of Commons, he began to write newspaper articles. This led to an offer from a

---

1. **humiliating** : making someone feel ashamed.
2. **shorthand** : stenography, a way of writing which uses signs to represent words or syllables.

publisher to write sketches for a monthly publication. The new series, which was published as *The Pickwick Papers*, established Dickens as a hugely popular writer.

Dickens was the most popular Victorian novelist and he became a public figure of considerable importance, despite his attacks on social problems. Dickens' early novel, *The Pickwick Papers*, which continued the 18th-century comic picaresque [1] tradition, was followed by *Oliver Twist* and *Nicholas Nickleby*, which were more serious novels. They attack both the treatment of the poor in Victorian England and the education system. Dickens continued his attacks on social institutions in *Bleak House* and *Little Dorrit*, where he criticised the legal system.

The focus of his comments in *A Christmas Carol*

1. **picaresque** : style of fiction dealing with the adventures of a rough and dishonest but appealing hero.

and *Hard Times* was slightly different. He was writing at the height of the Industrial Revolution, a period which saw, on the one hand, a great rise in living standards for many people, but on the other, great poverty and suffering in the new industrial cities. Dickens questioned whether the economic theories of the period could produce justice for the whole society.

Dickens is most remembered for the vast [1] collection of characters he created in his novels, rather than for his ideas about social policy. His focus was always on the individual, rather than on abstract [2] theories. He was, above all, a great stylist, and it was the quality of his writing that makes him popular with readers even today.

Dickens' most important novels include:

The Pickwick Papers, 1837; *Oliver Twist*, 1839; *Nicholas Nickleby*, 1839; *A Christmas Carol*, 1843; *Dombey and Son*, 1848; *David Copperfield*, 1850; *Bleak House*, 1853; *Hard Times*, 1854; *Little Dorrit*, 1857; *A Tale of Two Cities*, 1859; *Great Expectations*, 1861.

1 **Answer the following questions.**

    a. Why was Charles Dickens's father put in prison?

    b. What happened to Dickens after his father was sent to prison?

    c. What is one of the most important themes of Dickens's books?

    d. What was the name of his first popular book?

    e. What were the names of his next two novels?

    f. Why is Dickens still a popular writer?

1. **vast** : very large in quantity.   2. **abstract** : existing as an idea.

Before you read

FCE **1** **Listen to the first part of Chapter One and choose the best answer, (A, B or C).**

1. In what month does the opening scene take place?
   - A. ☐ November.
   - B. ☐ December.
   - C. ☐ September.

2. What were the guard and the driver afraid of?
   - A. ☐ the dark.
   - B. ☐ strange noises.
   - C. ☐ highwaymen.

3. How many passengers were there?
   - A. ☐ thirty.
   - B. ☐ three.
   - C. ☐ four.

4. What did the driver hear when they reached the top of the hill?
   - A. ☐ some highwaymen.
   - B. ☐ the passengers yelling.
   - C. ☐ a horse approaching.

5. What did the passengers see when they peered out?
   - A. ☐ a man on a horse.
   - B. ☐ a horse without a rider.
   - C. ☐ nothing.

6. Who does Mr Lorry work for?
   - A. ☐ the Dover mail.
   - B. ☐ a mademoiselle.
   - C. ☐ Tellson's Bank.

7. When did the mail arrive in Dover?
   - A. ☐ by the next evening.
   - B. ☐ by the next afternoon.
   - C. ☐ by the next morning.

8. Where had Mr Lorry come from?
   - A. ☐ London.
   - B. ☐ Paris.
   - C. ☐ Shooter's Hill.

Now read the text and check your answers.

CHAPTER ONE

Recalled to Life

The Dover mail [1] was struggling [2] up Shooter's Hill one November night in 1775. The road was dark and muddy and the passengers were all walking beside the coach to make the work of the horses easier. There were three passengers, all wearing heavy coats and boots. They trudged [3] wearily [4] up the hill through the heavy mist, not speaking to each other.

There was a great fear of highwaymen [5] in those days and the guard and driver of the Dover mail were anxious. They watched the passengers suspiciously. Just as the coach reached the top of the hill, the driver heard a noise in the darkness ahead. He listened intently [6] for a moment, then he was sure – there was a horse approaching at a gallop!

The guard had heard the noise as well and he drew out his

---

1. **Dover mail** : a coach that carried letters and passengers.
2. **struggling** : (here) moving with great difficulty.
3. **trudged** : walked with difficulty.
4. **wearily** : very tiredly.
5. **highwaymen** : armed robbers who attacked coaches.
6. **intently** : in an attentive way.

blunderbuss. [1] The passengers had also heard the horse and they stood in silence near the coach.

The sound of the horse was very clear and the guard called out loudly:

'Stop! Stop, or I'll fire!'

The rider stopped his horse very quickly. The passengers peered [2] uneasily [3] through the mist, but they could not see the rider or his horse.

'Is that the Dover mail?' the man on the horse called out.

The guard aimed [4] his weapon carefully.

'Why do you want to know?' he replied loudly.

'I want a passenger,' the voice replied. 'I'm looking for Mr Jarvis Lorry.'

One of the passengers stepped forward when he heard his name and spoke quickly to the guard. The guard looked suspiciously at Mr Lorry for a moment, then he called out to the rider again.

'Come closer to the coach,' he ordered. 'But come very slowly. If you move quickly, I'll fire!'

The man on the horse moved out of the darkness and approached the coach.

'It's all right, guard,' said Mr Lorry quietly. 'I work for Tellson's Bank in London and this man is one of our messengers.'

The messenger passed a piece of paper to Mr Lorry, who opened it hurriedly and read the message in the light of the coach lamp:

Wait at Dover for mademoiselle. [5]

Mr Lorry turned to the man on the horse.

'Jerry,' he ordered, 'take this answer back. "Recalled to life." They'll know what you mean. That's all. You can go now.'

---

1. **blunderbuss** : a very heavy gun.
2. **peered** : looked carefully because it is difficult to see clearly.
3. **uneasily** : anxiously, worriedly.
4. **aimed** : pointed.
5. **mademoiselle** : (title) Miss.

A Tale of Two Cities

Mr Lorry stepped into the coach and the driver flicked [1] his whip at the horses. The coach moved slowly forward towards Dover.

'"Recalled to life." That's the strangest message I've ever heard,' the man called Jerry said to himself. He paused for a moment or two, watching the coach disappear in the darkness and mist. Then he shrugged his shoulders and began the long ride back to London.

By morning the mail had arrived in Dover, stopping outside a hotel. Two of the passengers had got out previously at their destinations. Mr Lorry, the remaining passenger, climbed stiffly [2] down to the ground. He walked into the hotel and ordered breakfast. He was cold and hungry and he had not slept much during the long journey from London. He had been thinking a lot about the past, and his memories were painful ones. He sat by the fire and made himself comfortable. END

Mr Lorry ate his breakfast hungrily and then went outside for a walk. The coast of France could just be seen from the sea front at Dover. Mr Lorry peered anxiously towards it and his face grew serious. He plunged [3] into thought once more.

That afternoon Mr Lorry settled himself in the hotel. He ordered an early dinner and had just finished eating when he heard the sound of a carriage outside.

'That'll be mademoiselle!' he said to himself nervously.

A few minutes later the waiter came in to tell him that Miss Manette had arrived from London and that she wanted to see the gentleman from Tellson's Bank. Mr Lorry sighed deeply. He stood up and followed the waiter to Miss Manette's room in the hotel. He seemed a little afraid of meeting the young lady.

When he entered the room he saw a young girl of about seventeen standing near a table. The girl was slender [4] and she had

1. **flicked** : hit something with a short sudden movement.
2. **stiffly** : when you are stiff, your muscles hurt when you move them.
3. **plunged** : went deep.
4. **slender** : slim.

golden hair. Mr Lorry stared at her for a moment. He remembered an occasion many years before when he had carried a small child in his arms on the boat from France.

Miss Manette smiled at him.

'Please sit down, sir,' she said politely.

Mr Lorry sat down and waited for her to speak again.

'I had a message from Tellson's Bank yesterday,' Miss Manette went on. 'There is apparently some very surprising news about my father's property, which the bank said you would tell me about. The bank also told me I would have to travel to Paris to see about it. [1]

Mr Lorry nodded his head. For a moment there was silence and then he coughed awkwardly. [2]

'I am a man of business, Miss Manette. What I have to tell you is a matter of business. I want to tell you the story of one of our customers.'

Mr Lorry coughed again and then went on.

'This particular customer was a French gentleman – a doctor, as it happens.'

'Did he live in Beauvais?' Miss Manette asked eagerly.

'Yes he did. He lived in Beauvais – just like your father. I knew him, you see. I lived in Paris in those days and I worked in the Paris branch of Tellson's.'

'When did all this happen?' Miss Manette asked quickly.

'About twenty years ago,' Mr Lorry replied. 'The gentleman married an English lady and Tellson's Bank managed their financial affairs. It was a business relationship, you see – just a business relationship, you understand.'

'This is my father's story!' cried Miss Manette excitedly. She looked at Mr Lorry keenly, [3] as if trying to remember a face from

1. **to see about it** : to deal with it.
2. **awkwardly** : embarrassedly.
3. **keenly** : eagerly.

the past. 'Was it you who brought me to England after my parents died? Was it you, sir?'

Mr Lorry bowed to her politely.

'It was me,' he admitted. 'It was an affair of business, you see. Just business, that's all. As you have guessed, I am telling you the story of your father. You know that your father died, Miss Manette.' He coughed awkwardly again, as if he did not know how to go on with his story. 'But the man in my story did not die –'

Miss Manette went very pale. She began to tremble violently.

'Please be calm, my dear,' the banker said softly. He spoke gently now and he studied the young girl's face as he continued with his story. 'What if Monsieur Manette had not died? What if he had been taken away to a dreadful [1] place? What if he had had a powerful enemy who put him in prison? What if his friends did not know what had happened to him?'

Although Miss Manette was even paler now, she was listening to every word that the banker was saying.

'Go on, sir,' she said. 'Tell me everything – but tell me quickly!'

'Your father has been found, my dear. He is alive. He's been taken to the house of his old servant in Paris. That's why you and I are going to Paris!'

Miss Manette began to tremble even more than before.

'It won't be my father!' she cried in distress. [2] 'It will be his ghost. It's my father's ghost you're taking me to see, Mr Lorry – it's his ghost!'

Mr Lorry tried to calm the young girl.

'Nonsense, my dear,' he said softly. 'You're going to see your own father. The poor gentleman has suffered very badly, but you will bring him back to life.' Then he raised a hand in warning. 'We don't know what happened in the past,' he told her, 'and we

---

1. **dreadful** : terrible.　　2. **distress** : mental suffering.

mustn't ask. France is a dangerous country and our business is a secret one. I am carrying no papers with me at all. Our mission is a simple one, Miss Manette: "Recalled to life" describes it perfectly.'

Miss Manette looked at Mr Lorry. Her eyes were wide open and she was very pale. She did not say a word. She sat in perfect silence for a few minutes and Mr Lorry realised that she was in some kind of a faint. He shouted loudly for help.

A large, red-haired woman rushed into the room after Mr Lorry's call for help. She ran over to Miss Manette and seized her hand. Then she began to shout angrily at the hotel servants who had come into the room with her.

'Why don't you do something?' she yelled. 'Go and get some smelling salts [1] and some cold water. Don't just sit there looking at the poor girl!'

The servants ran out of the room to fetch [2] the things that were needed. The angry, red-haired woman bent tenderly over Miss Manette, stroking [3] her face and whispering softly to her. Then she turned to Mr Lorry in fury. [4]

'What have you done to her?' she asked angrily. 'Couldn't you give her your news without frightening her to death?'

Mr Lorry watched as the woman continued stroking Miss Manette's face and talking softly to her. After a few minutes the girl recovered consciousness.

'I hope she will be all right now,' Mr Lorry said quietly.

'No thanks to you!' the woman said fiercely.

---

1. **smelling salts** : strong-smelling chemicals used to revive people who had fainted.
2. **fetch** : collect.
3. **stroking** : moving a hand gently over.
4. **in fury** : in great anger.

Go back to the text

1 **Answer the following questions.**

a. Who was the man who appeared riding a horse?

b. What was the message that Mr Lorry gave to Jerry?

c. Why hadn't Mr Lorry slept during the journey?

d. What was Miss Manette like?

e. What part of her father's story did Miss Manette know before talking to Mr Lorry?

f. Why did Miss Manette begin to tremble violently?

g. What part of her father's story did Miss Manette know after talking to Mr Lorry?

h. Why did the red-haired woman get angry with Mr Lorry?

What's your opinion?

2 **Discuss the following questions with your friend(s).**

a. What was it about the way Mr Lorry told Miss Manette about her father that frightened her?

b. His way of telling Miss Manette about her father has a lot in common with the way a good storyteller works. Explain.

c. How would you have told Miss Manette about her father?

d. Mr Lorry works for a bank and is not a storyteller. Why do you think he told Miss Manette about her father in this fashion? [1]

e. Charles Dickens himself uses the same 'storytelling technique' as Mr Lorry in this first chapter. Find some examples.

---

1. **fashion** : manner.

Recalled to life

3 **Look at the following definitions of the verb 'to recall'.**

i. To remember something or bring something back to mind.

ii. To order somebody back from a place (often used in official contexts).

iii. To order something to be brought back (often used in official contexts).

1. **Say which of the three definitions explains the use of 'to recall' in the text.**

2. **Look at these six sentences with 'to recall' and say which definition applies.**

a. ☐ A large American automobile company recalled two of their car models because they had defective brakes.

b. ☐ Today France recalled its ambassadors in India because of a serious controversy with the Indian government.

c. ☐ I am sorry but I can't recall how to use this machine.

d. ☐ Her face looks quite familiar but I can't recall her name.

e. ☐ The New York Public Library is recalling all its books so it can count and update the list of all its books.

f. ☐ Senator Paganin was recalled to Washington to take part in an important debate.

The biggest shock in my entire life

 4 Later in life, Lucie decided to write about her exciting life. Pretend you are her and write in 120 - 180 words a description of the events described in this chapter. Include the following information:

- who your parents were
- how you came to England
- why you thought your father was dead
- what you thought when Mr Lorry called you to Dover
- Mr Lorry's strange way of telling you that your father was really alive
- why you forgave Mr Lorry in the end

You can begin and finish like this:

The biggest shock I ever had in my life was when...

So, in the end, I forgave Mr Lorry for having given me such a shock.

Before you go on

1 Listen to Chapter Two and decide who says the following:
M. Defarge (D), Miss Manette (M), Mr Lorry (L) or the old man (O).
Then read the chapter and check your answers.

a. ☐ He's locked in?

b. ☐ He has been a prisoner for many years.

c. ☐ Show the gentleman the shoes you are making.

d. ☐ Take a good look at him.

e. ☐ It's him.

f. ☐ Who are you?

g. ☐ We are going to England.

CHAPTER TWO

Paris

The streets in the Saint Antoine district of Paris were dirty and mean. [1] The people who lived there were poor, and most of them were thin and ill-fed. [2] A man was unloading a large barrel of wine from a cart in the street, when there was an accident. The barrel slipped out of the cart and broke in the street and a dark river of wine ran along the ground.

Stopping what they were doing, everyone ran to the spot [3] where the accident had taken place. Men, women and children began scooping up [4] the dirty wine and drinking it from their hands. There was laughter from the crowd as they scooped up the wine and there were smiles on the starved [5] faces of the people. Soon everyone's mouth and hands were stained red with the wine. One man dipped [6] his finger in the wine and scrawled [7] a dismal [8] word on the wall: BLOOD.

---

1. **mean** : narrow and ugly.
2. **ill-fed** : without enough to eat.
3. **spot** : place.
4. **scooping up** : taking with their hands.
5. **starved** : hungry.
6. **dipped** : put.
7. **scrawled** : wrote in an untidy and careless way.
8. **dismal** : miserable, depressing.

A Tale of Two Cities

Nearby there was a small wine shop and the owner was watching the scene in the street. He was a man of about thirty. He frowned [1] when he saw the joker write the word BLOOD on the wall. The wine shopkeeper's wife, Madame Defarge, was also watching the scene in the street. She, too, frowned, but she said nothing. She had some knitting [2] in her hands and her fingers worked continuously with the needles.

Monsieur [3] Defarge turned back into the shop after a few minutes. He was surprised that two customers had entered the shop unseen by him. One of them was a middle-aged gentleman and the other was a young girl. They were not the kind of people who would usually enter a wine shop in the Saint Antoine district. The gentleman said something quietly to Defarge. The wine shopkeeper was surprised for a moment, and then he signalled to the two customers to follow him out of the shop.

Mr Lorry and Miss Manette rose quickly from the table and followed Defarge. He led them through a little courtyard into another house. All three of them climbed the narrow staircase up to the top of the house. Defarge stopped outside a door and listened intently. He took a key out of his pocket.

'He's locked in?' exclaimed Mr Lorry in surprise. 'Why do you keep him locked in?'

'He has been a prisoner for many years,' Monsieur Defarge replied grimly, [4] 'and he would be frightened of freedom. That's why I always turn the key in the door when I go in.' **(E-1)** END

---

1. **frowned** : made a serious expression by bringing his eyebrows together.
2. **knitting** : clothing made from wool which is in the process of being made (knitted).
3. **Monsieur** : (title) Mr. or Sir.
4. **grimly** : very seriously.

Although Lucie Manette had not managed to hear any of the whispered conversation between the two men, she looked worried and frightened.

Defarge pushed the door open softly and they all entered the tiny, ill-lit room. There was an old man sitting with his back to the door. He was very busy making shoes.

Defarge made a slight noise and the old man turned to face him. He had long, white hair and an untidy beard, and he was very thin. The old man saw Miss Manette and Mr Lorry, but he showed no interest in them.

'Show the gentleman the shoes you are making,' Defarge commanded.

Mr Lorry stepped forward and leaned over the old man's work. Then he spoke quietly to him.

'Doctor Manette, don't you remember him?' he pointed at Defarge. 'Don't you remember your servant from long ago? Take a good look at him.'

The old man was startled [1] and dropped the shoe he was holding in his hand. He frowned for a moment, and it seemed as if he was struggling [2] to remember something from the past. The effort was too great for him, however, and after a few seconds his face went blank. [3] He reached down, picked up the shoe that had fallen, and resumed his work. [4]

'Do you recognise him, sir?' Defarge asked the Englishman.

'It's him,' Mr Lorry replied. 'He's greatly changed – but it is him.'

Miss Manette moved quietly to the old man's side and stood

1. **startled** : surprised and frightened.
2. **struggling** : making an attempt.
3. **blank** : without expression.
4. **resumed his work** : started his work again.

A Tale of Two Cities

beside him. She was still very pale, but there was an expression of great tenderness [1] on her face now. The old man raised his eyes and looked at her. He seemed afraid of her.

'What does this mean?' he asked fearfully. 'Who are you?'

He took hold of her long, golden hair and stroked it with his fingers. Then he began muttering [2] to himself.

'It's the same – but it's impossible. So much time has gone by. It's impossible!' He peered anxiously into her face. 'You can't be,' he said softly. 'You look like her and your hair is the same – but it's impossible. She would be old now, like me.'

Miss Manette put her arm around the old man and spoke softly to him.

'I am your daughter,' she told him gently, 'and I have come to take you home. We are going to England.'

---

1. **tenderness** : gentleness.
2. **muttering** : talking quietly and in a low voice.

Go back to the text

1 **Say whether the following sentences are True (T) or False (F), and then correct the false ones.**

		T	F
a.	The people who lived in the Saint Antoine district of Paris were mostly rich.	☐	☐
b.	When the barrel of wine broke in the street, everybody rushed to help the man who was unloading it.	☐	☐
c.	A man wrote the word 'blood' on a wall with the wine which had flowed onto the street.	☐	☐
d.	M. Defarge and his wife were not happy that someone had written the word 'blood' on the wall.	☐	☐
e.	Mr Lorry and Miss Manette entered M. Defarge's wine shop.	☐	☐
f.	M. Defarge locked Doctor Manette in his room because he did not want him to be afraid.	☐	☐
g.	When Doctor Manette first saw his daughter he did not react at all.	☐	☐
h.	M. Defarge was once Doctor Manette's servant.	☐	☐
i.	Mr Lorry had not seen Doctor Manette for many years.	☐	☐
j.	Miss Manette and Doctor Manette are now going to live in Paris.	☐	☐

Long time passing

2 **Answer the following questions.**

1. Who does Dr Manette think Lucie is?
2. Why does he think that?

The terror to come

3 Why is the scene with the wine barrel a kind of preview of the mob [1] violence that will occur during the French Revolution?
If you were a film director, how would you film the sequence of events in this chapter up to the point where we see Madame Defarge knitting?

Here are some filming terms to help you with your description.

- Close-up: filming from a short distance from the object.
- Medium shot: filming from a medium distance, i.e. from 2 to 10 metres.
- Long shot: filming from a long distance, i.e. from 10 metres or more.
- Tracking shot: filming with the camera moving; the camera can be on a cart that moves along.
- Panning shot: the camera turns around but stays in the same position.
- Overhead shot: filming from above the scene.

Plan the entire sequence which should last four minutes.

Example: Tracking shot along the street, showing the poor people and the general dirtiness. (20 seconds)
Long shot of man with cart and barrel of wine. (5 seconds)

1. **mob** : a large angry crowd.

Before you go on

 1 Read the text below and look carefully at each line. Some of the lines are correct, and some have a word which should not be there. If a line is correct put a tick (✓) opposite the number below. If a line has a word which should not be there, write the word. There are two examples at the beginning.

0.	Five years passed on. Doctor Manette and his daughter Lucie
00.	settled in a small house in London with Lucie's old nurse,
1.	Miss Pross. The doctor returned to health and began to see
2.	patients once more. Sometimes, however, memories of his
3.	suffering came back on to him and for a couple of days or
4.	more he would take up his shoe-making again. It was
5.	impossible to talk to him and he had lost all idea of where he
6.	was. He imagined himself to be back in prison and he
7.	withdrew himself completely into silence and suffering.
8.	Mr Lorry visited to them frequently when he had time off from
9.	his duties at Tellson's Bank, where Jerry Cruncher was still
10.	working as a messenger. One day the clerk told to Jerry to go
11.	straight away to the Old Bailey to deliver a message to Mr Lorry.
12.	'The Old Bailey, sir?' repeated Jerry. 'What's is going on there?
13.	And what's Mr Lorry have got to do with the Old Bailey, I
14.	wonder?'
15.	'Mr Lorry is giving evidence in a trial, that's all,' the clerk told
16.	him. Jerry hurried up to the Old Bailey as quickly as he could
17.	and entered into the grim old building. He pushed through the
18.	crowd of lawyers and spectators who had come for to watch
19.	the trial that was taking place.

0. ..on.. 00. ..✓.. 1. .... 2. .... 3. .... 4. .... 5. .... 6. ....
7. .... 8. .... 9. .... 10. .... 11. .... 12. .... 13. .... 14. ....
15. .... 16. .... 17. .... 18. .... 19. ....

 Now listen and check your answers.

CHAPTER THREE

The Old Bailey

Five years passed. Doctor Manette and his daughter Lucie settled [1] in a small house in London with Lucie's old nurse, Miss Pross. The doctor returned to health and began to see patients once more. Sometimes, however, memories of his suffering came back to him and for a couple of days or more he would take up his shoe-making again. It was impossible to talk to him and he lost all idea of where he was. He imagined himself to be back in prison and he withdrew completely into silence and suffering.

Mr Lorry visited them frequently when he had time off from his duties at Tellson's Bank, where Jerry Cruncher was still working as a messenger. One day the clerk told Jerry to go straight away to the Old Bailey [2] to deliver a message to Mr Lorry.

'The Old Bailey, sir?' repeated Jerry. 'What's going on there? And what's Mr Lorry got to do with the Old Bailey, I wonder?'

---

1. **settled** : made their home.
2. **Old Bailey** : famous court where serious criminal trials are held.

A Tale of Two Cities

'Mr Lorry is giving evidence in a trial, that's all,' the clerk told him.

Jerry hurried to the Old Bailey as quickly as he could and entered the grim [1] old building. He pushed through the crowd of lawyers and spectators who had come to watch the trial that was taking place. END

'What's the trial about?' he asked one of the officials. 'I suppose it's a forgery [2] case?'

'It's not forgery,' the official told him. 'It's more serious than that – it's treason!' [3]

'That's quartering,' [4] Jerry said quietly. 'Barbarous.' [5]

'It's the law,' the official said sternly.

E-2 Jerry made his way into the court and looked around for Mr Lorry. He saw him sitting next to an elderly gentleman and a young girl. They were talking seriously together and the young girl seemed worried and nervous. She kept looking towards the dock [6] where the prisoner was standing. The prisoner was a well-dressed young man. He stood calmly, waiting for the trial to begin.

The prosecuting counsel [7] rose to his feet and described the charges against the prisoner. The prisoner, he explained, was called Charles Darnay. He had travelled many times between England and France, and the prosecutor said that the purpose of his journeys was to carry information that was dangerous to England.

---

1. **grim** : ugly and depressing.
2. **forgery** : crime involving false documents or money.
3. **treason** : crime of doing something which betrays your country.
4. **quartering** : prisoners found guilty of treason were hanged until they were nearly unconscious, then they were pulled by horses, before being cut open with a knife.
5. **barbarous** : uncivilised.
6. **dock** : box where the defendant stands during a trial.
7. **prosecuting counsel** : a lawyer who tries to prove that a suspect is guilty.

A Tale of Two Cities

The prosecutor said that he would now bring forward his witnesses, who would prove that Charles Darnay was an enemy to England and that he deserved severe punishment. His first witness was a man called John Barsad. This witness said he had once been a friend of the prisoner's, but that he had broken off the friendship when he became sure that Charles Darnay was a spy [1] for France. The witness spoke confidently and the prosecuting counsel was obviously pleased with the way he gave his evidence.

Next it was the defence counsel's turn to ask John Barsad some questions. Had he ever been a spy himself? No. What was the source of his income? His property. Where was this property? He didn't remember. Had he ever been in prison? Never. Had he ever been in a debtor's prison? [2] Yes. How many times? Two or three. Not five or six? Perhaps. Had he ever been a gambler? No more than other gentlemen. Had he ever borrowed money from the prisoner? Yes. Had he paid the money back? No.

John Barsad left the witness stand a little awkwardly after the defence counsel had finished with him.

The prosecuting counsel called another witness, Mr Jarvis Lorry. He asked Mr Lorry to remember a night, five years ago, when he had been a passenger on the Dover mail.

'How many other passengers were there on the mail?'

'Two.'

'Was the prisoner one of them?'

'I don't know. They were both wrapped up against the cold – I could not see their faces.'

'Have you ever seen the prisoner anywhere?'

'Yes. He was on the boat when I returned from France a few days later.' **E-2** END

---

1. **spy** : a person who secretly gathers information about another country.
2. **debtor's prison** : a special kind of prison for people who owed money.

'Were you travelling alone, Mr Lorry?'

'No, I was travelling with Doctor Manette and his daughter Lucie.'

The prosecution counsel now called Lucie Manette to the stand. She confirmed that she had talked to the prisoner. Charles Darnay had noticed that her father was ill and had helped her to make the old man comfortable for the crossing. He had been polite and kind to both herself and her father. She hoped that her evidence would not get him into trouble.

The prosecution counsel now called a final witness to prove that Charles Darnay had got out of the Dover mail in the middle of the night, and had then walked some twelve miles through the darkness to a garrison town, [1] where he had waited for an accomplice. [2]

The prisoner's two defence counsels listened to this witness very carefully. The junior counsel, who had not played a very active part throughout the trial, yawned [3] and stretched in his chair, as if the whole trial was a bore and waste of time. Then he wrote a hurried note and passed it along to his colleague. His colleague read the note with surprise, then rose to his feet to ask the witness some questions.

'Are you quite sure that the man you saw in the garrison town was the prisoner, Charles Darnay?'

'Quite sure.'

'Have you ever seen anyone else who looked like the prisoner?'

'No.'

'Look at my young colleague for a moment,' the defence counsel told the witness. 'Now look at the prisoner again. Do they not look like each other?'

The witness looked at the young barrister. [4] Then he looked

---

1. **garrison town** : a town where there is an army camp.
2. **accomplice** : a person who helps others to do bad things.
3. **yawned** : opened the mouth wide to take a deep breath.
4. **barrister** : a lawyer who has the qualification to argue cases in the higher courts of law.

A Tale of Two Cities

again at the prisoner. It was true – the two men were similar.

'Can you still say that the man you saw in the garrison town was the prisoner?' asked the defence counsel.

The witness could not swear [1] it. It was possible he had made a mistake.

All the evidence had now been heard, and the jury retired to consider their verdict [2] on the prisoner. Everyone stood up and began to walk about the court, talking to friends and colleagues. The young defence counsel left his colleague for a moment and approached Mr Lorry.

'Is Miss Manette all right?' he asked eagerly, having seen her about to faint.

'She is upset, but she'll be all right,' Mr Lorry told him. 'You have given the prisoner a good defence, Mr Carton,' he said politely.

Sydney Carton smiled grimly. Then he walked up to the prisoner.

'Miss Manette will be all right,' he said coldly.

'I'm deeply sorry to have been the cause of her suffering,' Charles Darnay said.

Time moved slowly while the jury was considering the fate of the prisoner. Jerry was waiting outside the court building when Mr Lorry ran excitedly up to him, waving a piece of paper.

'Take this to the bank straight away,' he ordered.

Jerry looked at the piece of paper. There was one word written on it: ACQUITTED. [3]

'If he had written "Recalled to life", I would have understood him this time,' Jerry said to himself as he hurried towards Tellson's Bank.

1. **swear** : say something definitely.
2. **verdict** : decision reached by a jury.
3. **acquitted** : found innocent by the jury.

Go back to the text

FCE **1** Choose the correct answer (A, B, C or D).

1. Why did Doctor Manette sometimes begin making shoes again?
   - **A.** ☐ Because it relaxed him.
   - **B.** ☐ Because he sometimes thought that he was in prison again.
   - **C.** ☐ Because Lucie needed shoes.
   - **D.** ☐ Because it helped him not to think about his years in prison.

2. What was the trial which Mr Lorry was attending for?
   - **A.** ☐ forgery
   - **B.** ☐ murder
   - **C.** ☐ treason
   - **D.** ☐ bankruptcy

3. Why was Mr Lorry attending the trial?
   - **A.** ☐ He was a friend of the defendant's.
   - **B.** ☐ He was a witness of the crime.
   - **C.** ☐ He was giving evidence.
   - **D.** ☐ His bank had suffered from forgery.

4. Who was the person on trial?
   - **A.** ☐ Charles Darnay
   - **B.** ☐ Mr Lorry
   - **C.** ☐ John Barsad
   - **D.** ☐ Mr Carton

5. Precisely speaking, what was the prisoner accused of?
   - **A.** ☐ He had lent money to Mr Barsad.
   - **B.** ☐ He had gambled.
   - **C.** ☐ He had brought information to France which was dangerous to England.
   - **D.** ☐ He had brought information to England which was dangerous to France.

6. Why didn't Mr Lorry remember whether the prisoner had been on the Dover mail?

A. ☐ Because the other passengers had been covered up to keep warm.

B. ☐ Because it was such a long time ago.

C. ☐ Because it was dark outside.

D. ☐ Because his eyes are not very good, so he did not see the man on the mail very well.

7. Why was Lucie Manette worried about Charles Darnay?

A. ☐ Because he was French, like her.

B. ☐ Because he had been kind to her father when he was feeling ill.

C. ☐ Because he reminded her of Sydney Carton.

D. ☐ Because she was in love with him.

8. Why did the witness finally say that he could not swear that the man that he had seen in the garrison town was Charles Darnay?

A. ☐ Because it was very dark in the garrison town and he was no longer certain he had seen the witness.

B. ☐ Because he too thought that quartering was barbarous and he wanted no part in condemning a man to such a horrible death.

C. ☐ Because the man he thought was Charles Darnay was covered up against the cold wind of that night.

D. ☐ Because Charles Darnay looked like Sydney Carton, so he was no longer certain that he had seen Charles Darnay and not somebody else.

Interrogation

2 **Answer the following questions.**

a. What does the defence counsel imply is the real reason that John Barsad is accusing Charles Darnay?

b. Look at how Dickens presents the defence counsel's questioning of John Barsad. How is it different from the usual way of presenting a dialogue?

c. Look at how Dickens presents the prosecuting counsel's questioning of Mr Lorry. How is it different from the usual way of presenting a dialogue?

d. What is the effect that Dickens creates by using these two different techniques?

e. Think about films you have seen with courtroom scenes and the questioning of witnesses. How do film directors create similar effects?

Death is the remedy

3 Dickens wrote ironically, 'Death is Nature's remedy for all things, and why not Legislation's?' With regard to the period in which our story takes place, this was no exaggeration. Around 1789 in England, Parliament had decided that about 200 crimes could be punished by death, several of which are listed by Dickens at the beginning of the original version of *A Tale of Two Cities*, including:

- picking a pocket
- being found in the company of gypsies
- setting fire to a town
- setting fire to a pile of hay
- forgery
- writing a bad cheque
- counterfeiting a shilling coin (i.e. illegally making a shilling coin)

But execution could be even worse. Quartering, as Dickens tells us, meant that a man was 'half hanged' (i.e. not hanged until he was dead), and then the man was taken down and cut open; his inside organs were taken out and then burnt. All this, while the dying man was watching. Then his head was cut off, and his body was cut into quarters (four pieces).

Why do you think Dickens gives us this information about capital punishment [1] **in the beginning of his book about the horrors of the French Revolution?**

1. **capital punishment** : death penalty.

CHAPTER FOUR

Death and Revenge

Monseigneur was one of the great lords of France. He held a reception every fortnight [1] in the splendid surroundings of his Paris apartments. Before his guests arrived, Monseigneur's servants brought him his chocolate to drink. It took four men to prepare Monseigneur's morning chocolate. The first man carried the chocolate, the second stirred it, the third presented Monseigneur with the napkin [2] and the fourth poured out the chocolate.

Many important people came to Monseigneur's reception and they all had requests to make of him. One of his visitors was the Marquis of Evrémonde, an elegant man in his sixties. Monseigneur did not like the Marquis, and although he was courteous [3] to him, it was clear that the Marquis was out of favour. [4]

The Marquis of Evrémonde left the reception in a bad temper. He entered his carriage and told his man to drive away quickly. The carriage rattled [5] swiftly through the busy streets and people

---

1. **fortnight** : a period of two weeks.
2. **napkin** : a square piece of cloth used to clean your mouth and hands.
3. **courteous** : polite.

4. **out of favour** : not popular with the authorities.
5. **rattled** : moved noisily.

Death and Revenge

got out of its way as best they could to avoid being run over.

Soon the carriage was rattling through the Saint Antoine district of Paris. The Marquis looked out of the window in disgust at the poverty of the area. Suddenly there was a crash and the carriage came to a halt. [1] 'What's the matter?' the Marquis asked the driver.

It appeared that the carriage had run over a child in the street. The child was dead and the father could be heard crying and shrieking [2] in grief. [3]

'You people should be more careful,' the Marquis said to the crowd who were standing around the carriage. 'How do I know you haven't hurt one of my horses?'

Defarge, the wine shop owner, was there. He stepped forward to the father and tried to comfort him.

'Be brave, Jacques,' he said. 'It is better for the child to die now, than to live as we do.'

The Marquis heard the wine shopkeeper's words and he leaned out of the carriage to look at him.

'You are a philosopher,' he said. He took a coin out of his pocket and flung [4] it carelessly on the ground. 'Spend that as you like,' he cried contemptuously, [5] and then he waved at the servant to drive on. The carriage began to move through the streets once more.

The Marquis had just settled himself comfortably on the cushions when the coin he had flung to Defarge was suddenly hurled [6] into the carriage.

'Stop!' the Marquis cried out angrily to the servant.

He looked out of the carriage window to see where Defarge was, but there was no sign of the wine shopkeeper. He could only see the

---

1. **came to a halt** : stopped moving.
2. **shrieking** : screaming.
3. **grief** : extreme sadness.
4. **flung** : threw.
5. **contemptuously** : arrogantly and rudely.
6. **hurled** : thrown with great force.

A Tale of Two Cities

distraught [1] father and the crowd of poor people looking at him.

'You dogs!' he said smoothly. [2] 'If I knew who had thrown that coin, I'd crush him under the wheels.' He turned to his servant. 'Go on!' he cried.

It was evening before the Marquis's fine carriage reached the historic chateau [3] where he lived. The last few miles of the journey took the Marquis through the village near the chateau. The village was a poor one and the people who lived in it looked badly fed and unhappy. The Marquis ordered the servant to stop the carriage in the village centre. Then he looked out of the window and called one of the men over.

'I passed you on the road outside the village,' the Marquis said. 'Why did you look at the carriage in the way you did?'

'It was the man, sir,' the villager replied humbly.

'What man, you fool?'

'There was a man underneath the carriage, sir,' the villager explained. 'He was hanging on to the chains.'

'Who was he?' the Marquis asked. 'You know everyone around here. Who was the man?'

'I don't know, sir,' the man replied. 'I've never seen him before.'

'You saw a thief hanging under the carriage and you didn't say anything,' the Marquis said quietly. 'Gabelle!' he called.

Monsieur Gabelle was the village postmaster. He collected taxes from the villagers and was one of the Marquis's most loyal servants. He came running forward eagerly.

'Yes, sir,' he cried.

'If you find this mysterious man who was travelling under the carriage, I want you to arrest him — is that clear?'

Monsieur Gabelle bowed deeply.

'It will be done, sir,' he assured the Marquis.

The Marquis was soon sitting in front of a supper-table in the

---

1. **distraught** : very unhappy.
2. **smoothly** : calmly.
3. **chateau** : a large house.

Death and Revenge

chateau. The table was laid for two people, but the Marquis was alone.

'Has my nephew arrived yet?' the Marquis asked his servant.

'Not yet, sir,' the servant replied.

The Marquis lifted a wine glass to his lips and then he listened intently.

'What was that?' he asked, pointing to the window. 'Open the window.'

The servant opened the window and leaned out. He listened for a moment and then he turned back to the Marquis.

'There's nothing, sir,' he said. 'Just the wind in the trees.'

The Marquis shrugged [1] and went on with his dinner. A few minutes later he paused once more, listening. This time he could hear a carriage drawing up [2] at the chateau. A servant came in to announce that the Marquis's nephew had arrived.

The man known as Charles Darnay in London entered the room. He bowed politely to the Marquis, who returned the bow coldly.

'Have you come from London?' the Marquis asked.

'Yes, sir, from London,' Charles Darnay confirmed. 'I have had difficulties there, as I'm sure you know. Perhaps you were the cause of some of those difficulties?' he hinted. [3]

'No, no, no,' his uncle said cheerfully.

'I know you would do anything to stop me,' Charles Darnay went on, 'and I know you have no scruples.' [4]

'I did warn you,' his uncle replied.

'I remember,' Charles Darnay confirmed. 'It's a good thing for me that you're out of favour at Court, or I believe you'd use your powers to have me imprisoned through the old device of a *lettre de*

---

1. **shrugged** : made a dismissive movement with his shoulders.
2. **drawing up** : stopping.
3. **hinted** : suggested.
4. **scruples** : moral principles.

cachet.' [1]

The Marquis smiled icily.

'I might do many things for the honour of the family,' he agreed. 'But you are right, I am out of favour at court.' He paused for a moment to think and then he went on. 'The aristocracy [2] has lost a great deal of its power, but I shall do whatever I can to protect our family from further losses.'

'Ours is the most hated name in France,' Charles Darnay told him. 'The people in the village have no respect for us – they are simply afraid.'

'They have to be afraid of us,' his uncle said firmly. 'Fear makes them obey and I require their obedience.'

'Our family has done wrong,' Charles Darnay said. 'We've been cruel. We have injured anyone who threatened our pleasure. Our system is a rotten one. I promised my mother when she was dying that I would have nothing to do with it. I have given up the Evrémonde title and when the time comes I shall give up all the property as well.'

'How do you live in England?' the Marquis asked.

'I work for my living, sir,' Charles Darnay said with dignity. [3]

Again the Marquis smiled with contempt.

'I hear you have made friends in England,' he said. 'Do you know a certain Frenchman, a doctor and his daughter?'

'Doctor Manette? Yes, I know him and his daughter,' Charles Darnay replied in surprise.

'But now it's late,' the Marquis remarked. 'We can talk again in the morning. I wish you good night, dear Charles.'

Darnay bowed once more and left his uncle alone. The Marquis sneered [4] when he was alone. Soon after, he retired to bed. He lay on

---

1. ***lettre de cachet*** : aristocrats could have their enemies imprisoned without trial if they could obtain a *lettre de cachet* from a government minister.

2. **aristocracy** : nobility.

3. **dignity** : quality that earns respect.

4. **sneered** : made a face expressing displeasure and contempt.

Death and Revenge

a large and luxurious bed and closed his eyes. The hours of the night went by. The horses in the stables [1] moved restlessly, the dogs barked, and somewhere an owl screeched. [2]

The sun rose and people in the village began to come out of their houses. Nothing moved in the chateau. Suddenly the silence was broken by the ringing of the chateau's great bell and a servant on horseback appeared in the village. The servant went to Monsieur Gabelle's house. A few minutes later Monsieur Gabelle came out of the house and ran up to the chateau.

The cause of all this excitement was soon clear. The Marquis lay on his fine bed with a dagger [3] through his heart. There was a note attached to the murder weapon:

Drive him fast to his tomb. JACQUES.

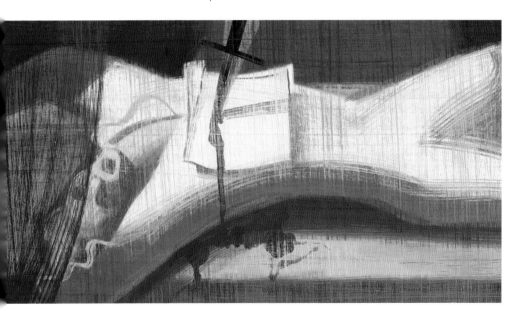

1. **stables** : buildings where horses are kept.
2. **screeched** : cried out noisily.
3. **dagger** : a short pointed knife.

Go back to the text

FCE 1 Chapter Four has been divided into nine parts. Choose the most suitable heading from the list A-J for each part 1-9 of the text. There is one extra title which you do not need to use. The first one has been done for you.

- **A** ☐ A job's better than a bad name
- **B** ☐ Don't stand in my way
- **C** ☐ The stranger below
- **D** ☐ Anything for the family
- **E** ☐ The cruel end of a cruel man
- **F** ☐ As easy as one, two, three
- **G** ☐ Even the poor don't want his money
- **H** 1 An unwelcome guest
- **I** ☐ Money for your thought
- **J** ☐ Unwanted even at home

An indictment [1] of the French aristocracy

2 Answer the following questions.

a. How does Dickens use satire [2] to condemn the French aristocracy?

b. The Marquis looked at the scenes of poverty with disgust, and certainly Dickens looked at poverty with disgust too. How, then, are their points of view different?

1. **indictment** : condemnation.
2. **satire** : a way of criticizing people in a funny way.

Summing it all up

3 **Number the paragraphs in the right order to make a summary of the first four chapters, and then fill in the gaps with the words given below.**

> faint   blunderbuss   acquitted   recalled
> chateau   England   mail   tremble   condemned
> spy   dagger   mist   shoes   give   drive
> evidence   highwaymen   rotten   wife   father
> health   treason   certain
> Marquis   mademoiselle   wine shop

a. ☐ Five years later, Lucie and her father, who had now returned to 1........................, lived in England; and Mr Lorry often visited them. It was in this period that both Lucie and Mr Lorry were called to give 2........................ at a 3........................ trial. The man on trial was named Charles Darnay, and he was suspected of being a French 4........................ because he often travelled back and forth between England and France.

b. ☐ Mr Lorry and Lucie Manette went to the Saint Antoine district of Paris to the 5........................ of a certain Monsieur Defarge. He took them up to a locked door, which he then unlocked. Inside was an old man making 6........................ . Mr Lorry recognised him, but the old man was lost in his own private world. He even thought that Lucie was his dead 7........................ . Lucie had to tell him that she was his daughter and that she was taking him back to 8........................ .

c. ☐ The next morning the 9........................ arrived in Dover and Mr Lorry went to the hotel for breakfast. Then that evening the 10........................ arrived. Her name was Miss Manette, and Mr Lorry went to see her in her room. He began to tell her

47

about a little girl he had brought to England from France twenty years earlier.

d. 1 Mr Lorry and two other passengers were walking up a hill beside the Dover mail through a heavy [11]........................... when they heard a horse galloping towards them. The guard pulled out his [12]........................... because they were all afraid of [13]........................... . Fortunately it was a messenger named Jerry from Tellson's Bank with a message for Mr Lorry. It told him to wait at Dover for mademoiselle. Mr Lorry then gave the messenger a message to take back; it said, '[14]........................... to life'.

e. ☐ After the trial, Charles Darnay, who was a member of the French nobility, returned to his family home, a historic [15]........................... in France. There his uncle, the cruel [16]........................... Evrémonde, was waiting for him. Charles did not like his uncle at all and he even thought that he might have been responsible for his trial.

f. ☐ He was not very clear in his story but soon she understood that he was talking about her [17]........................... and herself. Miss Manette began to [18]........................... and then she was silent. Mr Lorry realised that she was in a [19]........................... and called for a servant.

g. ☐ They then talked about their family. Charles explained how he had promised his mother that he would [20]........................... up the family name and how he did not want to be part of the family because he thought that their way of life was [21]........................... . People obeyed them out of fear, not out of respect. Charles then left his uncle and went to bed. That very night, though, the Marquis Evrémonde was killed in his bed. A servant found him with a [22]........................... through his heart, and a note that said, '[23]........................... *him fast to his tomb. JACQUES.*'

h. ☐ It seemed that the accused would be [24]........................... until a young barrister working for the defence named Sydney Carton had an idea. He told one of his colleagues to ask one of the key witnesses whether the prisoner looked like Sydney Carton. The witness said that he did. This meant that the witness could no longer be [25]........................... that the man he saw in a garrison town was really Charles Darnay and not somebody who looked like him. So, thanks to Sydney Carton, Charles Darnay was [26]........................... .

Before you go on

FCE 1 **Read the text below and think of the word which best fills each space. Use only one word in each space. There is an example at the beginning (0).**

More time passed and Mr Charles Darnay established himself in England (0)............as............ a teacher of French. He often visited Doctor Manette and Lucie, and gradually he fell (1)........................... love. Mr Lorry was a visitor to the house as well, going there (2)........................... Sundays after his week's work at Tellson's Bank.

The young lawyer Sydney Carton (3)........................... another visitor at Doctor Manette's house. He was a strange young man, often bitter and sharp in his conversation. He drank too much and (4)........................... was an air of sadness about him. He (5)........................... not like Charles Darnay and was frequently cold in his behaviour to the Frenchman (6)........................... life he had so brilliantly saved at the Old Bailey.

Charles Darnay finally managed to approach Doctor Manette to tell (7)........................... of his love for Lucie. The old man did not want to lose (8)........................... daughter, but he liked Darnay and respected him.

'If my daughter loves you,' he told the young man, 'I shall
(9)............................ happy to see you married to her.'

'There's one other thing,' Darnay added. 'You know that my name is
not really Darnay. I'd rather you knew (10)............................ I really
am.'

'No!' cried Doctor Manette suddenly. (11)............................ a
moment he looked quite afraid. 'I don't wish to hear it now, my
friend. But you (12)............................ tell me,' he went on, 'on the
morning (13)............................ the day you marry Lucie.'

A few days (14)............................ Sydney Carton came to the house.
He looked tired and ill and appeared to be ashamed of himself.

'Are you all right?' Lucie asked him.

'No, Miss Manette,' he replied sadly. 'I lead a bad life and I am never
all right. But what can be (15)............................?'

 Now listen to the first part of Chapter Five to check your answers.

CHAPTER FIVE

A Marriage and a Confession

More time passed and Mr Charles Darnay established himself in England as a teacher of French. He often visited Doctor Manette and Lucie, and gradually he fell in love. Mr Lorry was a visitor to the house as well, going there on Sundays after his week's work at Tellson's Bank.

The young lawyer Sydney Carton was another visitor at Doctor Manette's house. He was a strange young man, often bitter [1] and sharp [2] in his conversation. He drank too much and there was an air of sadness about him. He did not like Charles Darnay and was frequently cold in his behaviour to the Frenchman whose life he had so brilliantly saved at the Old Bailey.

Charles Darnay finally managed to approach Doctor Manette to tell him of his love for Lucie. The old man did not want to lose his daughter, but he liked Darnay and respected him.

---

1. **bitter** : unhappy and angry.
2. **sharp** : critical.

A Tale of Two Cities

'If my daughter loves you,' he told the young man, 'I shall be happy to see you married to her.'

'There's one other thing,' Darnay added. 'You know that my name is not really Darnay. I'd rather you knew who I really am.'

'No!' cried Doctor Manette suddenly. For a moment he looked quite afraid. 'I don't wish to hear it now, my friend. But you can tell me,' he went on, 'on the morning of the day you marry Lucie.'

A few days later Sydney Carton came to the house. He looked tired and ill and appeared to be ashamed of himself.

'Are you all right?' Lucie asked him.

'No, Miss Manette,' he replied sadly. 'I lead a bad life and I am never all right. But what can be done?' END

E-4 'You could change your way of living, perhaps,' Lucie suggested with a smile.

She was surprised to see tears coming to his eyes.

'It's too late for that,' he told her. 'I shall go on living the way I do and I shall sink lower and lower. I can't help it.' He paused and looked embarrassed. 'Please forgive me for talking like this to you,' he said humbly. 'I shall never do it again, but I have something particular that I want to say to you.' Again he paused and looked at her in great distress. 'I have loved you from the first,' he said, 'and the thought of you has made me try to change my life. But it's useless – it's too late to change.'

'It's never too late to change,' Lucie suggested softly.

'I shall go on living the way I do,' he said, 'but I shall always love you. I will sink lower and lower in life, but my heart will always be turned to you. And if there is ever anything I can do for you, or for the people that you love, I would do it – no matter the cost!'

One evening Doctor Manette and his daughter were sitting together in the garden. Lucie was to be married the following day.

'You won't feel lonely when I'm married, will you father?' Lucie asked anxiously.

A Marriage and a Confession

'I've already told you,' her father replied calmly, 'that your marriage to Charles gives me great pleasure. He's a fine young man, my dear – and I'm happy for both of you.'

The old man was very thoughtful as he went up to his room that night. He had pretended to be happy, but his mind was troubled [1] by his daughter's marriage. He was afraid of loneliness.

The next morning Charles Darnay came to the house. He had not forgotten his promise to Doctor Manette and had come to tell the old man his real name. He and the doctor went into the study together, where they remained for a few minutes.

When they came out, the doctor looked pale and he was trembling. He made a great effort, however, and managed to look cheerful and happy during the wedding ceremony. **E-4** END

---

1. **troubled** : disturbed.

A Tale of Two Cities

Lucie and her husband left London on their honeymoon. Doctor Manette, Miss Pross and Mr Lorry said goodbye to them. The doctor was very quiet and thoughtful for the rest of the day and Mr Lorry was worried about him.

'I must go to Tellson's Bank,' Mr Lorry told Miss Pross, 'but I'll come back as soon as I've finished there.'

It was evening before Mr Lorry returned to the house. He entered the doctor's room and found the old man standing at a table with his back to the door. He was making shoes, just as he had been doing when Mr Lorry found him in Paris!

Mr Lorry spoke quietly to the doctor but he received no reply. The doctor did not recognise him.

Miss Pross and Mr Lorry watched the doctor carefully over the next few days. They did not want to ruin [1] Lucie's honeymoon by telling her that her father was ill. They hoped he would recover before the young couple came home. The days passed slowly and Doctor Manette spent them making shoes.

On the tenth day, however, there was a change in the doctor's condition. He came downstairs in the morning in the usual way and he talked normally to Miss Pross and Mr Lorry. He had recovered completely, but he had no memory of the days he had spent making shoes.

---

1. **ruin** : spoil the enjoyment of something.

Go back to the text

1 **Answer the following questions.**

a. What kind of work did Charles Darnay do in England?

b. What was Sydney Carton like?

c. How did Doctor Manette react when Charles Darnay said that he wanted to tell him his real name?

d. Why did Sydney Carton say that he was so sad?

e. What did Sydney Carton say that he was willing to do for Lucie?

f. How did Doctor Manette react immediately after he discovered Charles' real name?

Self-sacrifice

 2 1. **Sydney Carton shows his love for Lucie by doing something which is good for her but difficult for him. What does he do?**

2. **Pretend that you are Sydney Carton and in 120-180 words describe what you have done for Lucie and why it was so difficult.**

Include:

• How he met Lucie.

• His opinion of Charles Darnay.

• How he feels about the wedding of Charles and Lucie.

• Why he feels that he could never be a good husband for Lucie.
(Charles Dickens never really tells us what Sydney Carton has done that is so bad; all that we know is that he drinks too much, that he defends criminals and that he knows the corrupt world of the law courts of the Old Bailey extremely well.)

• How he felt and what he did after he decided that he could not marry Lucie.

You can begin like this:

I fell in love with Lucie Manette the first time I saw her in

....

....

....

....

....

....

....

....

Even if I am unworthy of Lucie, I hope that my love for her
will some day help her to lead a happy life.

Before you go on

1 **Fill in the gaps with the words given, and then listen to the first part of Chapter Six to check your answers.**

> news   wine   customers   night   happening   Paris
> Bastille   Mr Lorry   soon   Defarge   valuables
> Sydney Carton   sea   swords   went

Another six years ¹......................... by and Lucie and Charles Darnay
were happy together. They now had a young daughter, also called
Lucie. Doctor Manette had never fallen into his illness again and he,
too, was cheerful and contented. ²......................... continued his
Sunday visits to the household and was regarded as one of the
family. ³......................... visited the family as well, but only came
five or six times a year. He took care never to drink ⁴.........................
on the days when he came to the house.

One ⁵......................... in July 1789, Mr Lorry came to the house after
he had finished work at Tellson's Bank. He seemed tired.

'It's been a busy day,' he said. 'Our 6......................... in France are uneasy. Our Paris office has been full of customers and all of them have been leaving their money and 7......................... for us to look after. They all want their property sent to England as 8......................... as possible.'

'The situation in France is serious,' commented Charles Darnay. 'The 9......................... from there is not good.'

There was much excitement in the Saint Antoine district of 10......................... that day. Many people could be seen in the streets. Most of them were carrying weapons. 11......................... was issuing orders to the men who stood near him. His face was determined and solemn.

'Keep near me, Jacques Three,' he told one of the men. Then he turned to the crowd and roared, 'To the 12.........................!'

There was a huge cheer from the people in the street. 13......................... were waved and muskets loaded. There was soon a 14......................... of people surrounding the Bastille prison and clamouring for entry. A few soldiers leaned down from the Bastille walls to see what was 15......................... .

CHAPTER SIX

The Revolution in France

Another six years went by and Lucie and Charles Darnay were happy together. They now had a young daughter, also called Lucie. Doctor Manette had never fallen into his illness again and he, too, was cheerful and contented. Mr Lorry continued his Sunday visits to the household and was regarded as one of the family. Sydney Carton visited the family as well, but only came five or six times a year. He took care never to drink wine on the days when he came to the house.

One night in July 1789, Mr Lorry came to the house after he had finished work at Tellson's Bank. He seemed tired.

'It's been a busy day,' he said. 'Our customers in France are uneasy. [1] Our Paris office has been full of customers and all of them have been leaving their money and valuables [2] for us to look after. They all want their property sent to England as soon as possible.'

'The situation in France is serious,' commented Charles Darnay. 'The news from there is not good.'

---

1. **uneasy** : worried.
2. **valuables** : things which worth a lot of money.

The Revolution in France

* * * *

There was much excitement in the Saint Antoine district of Paris that day. Many people could be seen in the streets. Most of them were carrying weapons. Defarge was issuing [1] orders to the men who stood near him. His face was determined and solemn.

'Keep near me, Jacques Three,' he told one of the men. Then he turned to the crowd and roared, [2] 'To the Bastille!'

There was a huge cheer from the people in the street. Swords were waved and muskets [3] loaded. [4] There was soon a sea of people surrounding the Bastille prison and clamouring [5] for entry. A few soldiers leaned down from the Bastille walls to see what was happening.

Orders were shouted and the crowd attacked the Bastille. There was fire and smoke everywhere and in the centre stood Defarge, always directing his men to the enemy's weakest places.

'Forward!' he cried.

Madame Defarge was also there, commanding the women of Paris who took part in the battle.

'We can kill as well!' she cried as she led the women forward.

The defenders of the Bastille were soon swept away and the governor of the prison was set upon [6] and killed by the angry crowd. Defarge led his men into the building and they liberated [7] the prisoners. Then he made his way to the cell that had once been Doctor Manette's. He peered at the walls and the few pieces of furniture. He was looking for something.

'Look, Jacques!' he cried excitedly. 'Look there, on the wall!'

He pointed at some initials: [8] A.M.

---

1. **issuing** : giving out, emitting.
2. **roared** : shouted loudly.
3. **muskets** : old-fashioned firearms.
4. **loaded** : (here) filled with bullets.

5. **clamouring** : demanding loudly.
6. **set upon** : attacked.
7. **liberated** : freed.
8. **initials** : the first letters of a name.

A Tale of Two Cities

'Alexandre Manette,' he said. 'This was the doctor's cell, all right.'

He began to search the old fireplace, dislodging [1] a cloud of dust as he did so. Something fell into the fireplace and Defarge bent quickly to pick it up.

'There's nothing here, Jacques,' he said. 'We may as well go.'

* * * *

Mr Lorry was constantly busy at Tellson's Bank because of the dramatic [2] events in France. There was a continuous stream of customers from France in the bank's premises, [3] and people left messages for friends and family members there.

One day Charles Darnay happened to visit Mr Lorry in his office. Mr Lorry was preparing to travel to France on business. Darnay tried to persuade him not to go, pointing out the dangers of such a trip while the country was undergoing [4] a revolution.

'Don't try to dissuade [5] me,' the banker said with a smile. 'I've worked for Tellson's all my life and I feel a loyalty to the bank and to our customers. I must go!'

Just then one of the bank's clerks brought in a letter and handed it to Mr Lorry.

'This has come for the Marquis St. Evrémonde, sir,' the clerk explained. 'But no one knows where the Marquis is – or even if he's in England at all.'

Charles Darnay, who had inherited [6] the title from his uncle, had kept the truth of his identity a secret from everybody except Doctor Manette. He did not want to reveal it to Mr Lorry.

'As it happens,' he told Mr Lorry, 'I know the Marquis. I'll deliver the letter for you, if you like.'

---

1. **dislodging** : knocking loose.
2. **dramatic** : impressive, sudden and often surprising.
3. **premises** : (here) the buildings that a bank uses.
4. **undergoing** : experiencing.
5. **dissuade** : persuade someone not to do something.
6. **inherited** : received.

The Revolution in France

Mr Lorry was happy to pass the letter to him.

Later that day Darnay opened the letter from France. He read it with trembling hands:

Dear Marquis,

I have always been a faithful servant to the Evrémonde family and now I have been arrested and thrown into prison in Paris. They tell me I am an enemy of the people and that I must die. My crime is that I followed your orders after your uncle died. I beg you to come to France and help your old servant,

Gabelle

Darnay had made his decision before he finished reading this appeal for help. He knew that he had to go to France to do what he could for Gabelle. He sighed deeply. He did not want to leave Lucie and Doctor Manette, but he knew that he had to go. He wrote a letter to Lucie explaining why he had to travel to Paris and then he left for France.

Go back to the text

1 **Say whether the following statements are True (T) or False (F), and then correct the false ones.**

		T	F
a.	After Lucie married, her father fell ill more and more often.	☐	☐
b.	Mr Lorry visited Lucie and Charles few times during the year.	☐	☐
c.	Sydney Carton often came drunk to visit Lucie and Charles Darnay.	☐	☐
d.	Monsieur Defarge followed the angry crowd to the Bastille prison.	☐	☐
e.	Monsieur Defarge and other women watched the furious attack on the Bastille prison.	☐	☐
f.	Monsieur Defarge went to the cell in the Bastille where Doctor Manette had been a prisoner for many years.	☐	☐
g.	Monsieur Defarge did not find anything in Doctor Manette's cell.	☐	☐
h.	In July of 1789 the French customers of Tellson's Bank wished to send their money and valuables to England.	☐	☐
i.	Mr Lorry gave Charles Darnay the letter for the Marquis St. Evrémonde because he knew that was his real name.	☐	☐
j.	The letter to the Marquis was from one of his servants who was in prison.	☐	☐
k.	Charles Darnay wanted to help his servant but he could not leave Lucie.	☐	☐
l.	Mr Lorry went to France to help Gabelle.	☐	☐

Past Perfect

'Then he made his way to the cell that had once been Doctor Manette's.'

In English we use the Past Simple to talk about past events.
*He **arrived** in Paris.*

The Past Perfect, which is formed with **had** + past participle, is used to talk about an event that happened before that point in time.
*When he arrived in Paris, Charles **had** already **returned** to London.*

Look at the difference in meaning between these two sentences:
*When Mr Lorry **arrived** Charles **left**.* = Mr Lorry arrived and then Charles left.

*When Mr Lorry **arrived** Charles **had left**.* = Mr Lorry arrived but Charles had already left.

2 Match the sentences in Column A with the sentences in Column B on page 66 to form true sentences using the Past Perfect and *because*. You must decide which event happened before the other. The first one has been done for you.

Column A

1. [e] the revolution begin there
2. [ ] Miss Manette recognise Mr Darnay at the trial
3. [ ] his servant Gabelle write him a letter
4. [ ] Doctor Manette look pale
5. [ ] Mr Lorry wait at Dover
6. [ ] he fall out of favour with the court
7. [ ] her father disappear
8. [ ] someone kill the Marquis
9. [ ] Jacques cry
10. [ ] there be the initials A.M. on the wall
11. [ ] Charles give up the Evrémonde title
12. [ ] She think her father was dead

Column B

a. Charles Darnay decide to travel to Paris

b. his family do many cruel things

c. the Marquis of Evrémonde not be able to obtain *lettre de cachet* against Charles

d. Mr Lorry bring Lucie to England

e. it be dangerous to travel to France

f. there be a lot of excitement around the castle

g. Charles tell him his real name

h. it be Doctor Manette's cell

i. he receive a message from his bank

j. Miss Manette faint

k. Marquis kill his child

l. she see him on the boat returning from France

1. It was dangerous to travel to France because the revolution had begun there.

2. ....

3. ....

4. ....

5. ....

6. ....

7. ....

8. ....

9. ....
   ....

10. ....
    ....

11. ....
    ....

12. ....
    ....

Poverty, crime and the law

3 Often poverty and crime go together, and at times the law arrives where there is crime. In any case, in this crossword puzzle you will find words that concern all three.

Across

4. The name of the man accused of treason.
7. A large, heavy gun.
11. A short pointed knife used to stab people.
12. The ... counsel tries to have the defendant condemned.
16. The formal examination in a court to decide if a person is innocent or guilty.
19. Helping the enemies of your country.
21. One form of ... for committing a crime is prison.
22. Those men who robbed people travelling on roads.

Down

1. The illegal killing of a person.
2. Accusations against a defendant.
3. Somebody who is employed by a country to obtain information from an enemy country.
5. The defence ... tries to keep his client from being condemned.
6. A punishment where they cut your body into four parts at the end of horrible torture.

8. Another name for a lawyer in England. This one can represent a client in a higher court of law.
9. The area in a court where the accused stands.
10. The nickname for the central criminal court in London is The Old ...
13. If the person accused of a crime is found innocent he is ...
14. In a poor area you will see many ... faces, i.e., thin faces because the people don't have enough to eat.
15. The person who sees a crime being committed.
17. The crime of illegally copying something, such as somebody else's signature.
18. Depressing.
20. Something you use for hurting or killing such as knives, guns, bombs, etc.

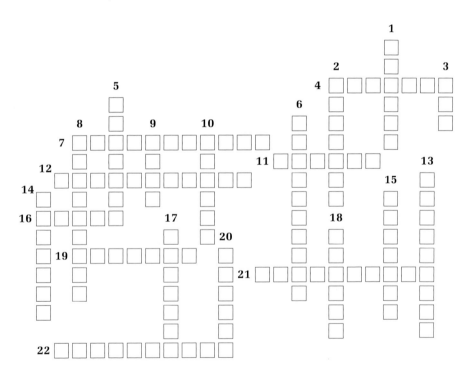

THE FRENCH REVOLUTION

The Causes of the French Revolution

Until the Revolution, France had been an absolute [1] monarchy. [2] The power of the king was not limited by a Parliament or Assembly. French society was divided into three large groups, known as the 'estates' – the clergy, [3] the nobility and the bourgeoisie. [4] The clergy and nobility were exempt from taxation.

The taxation system brought France close to bankruptcy [5] in the 18th century. The system was hated by the bourgeoisie and peasantry, [6] who had to pay for government inefficiency and corruption.

France had sent soldiers to support Washington's army in America. The soldiers returned to France with some of the ideas of the American struggle for independence from Britain. The most important of these revolutionary ideas were the right to take up arms against tyranny, [7] no taxation without representation, and the rights of man.

There was general discontent in 1788. The nobles and clergy feared the introduction of a new system of taxation. The bourgeoisie wanted a greater role in the economic and political life of the country. The peasantry wanted a more equal and fairer society.

Louis XVI tried to deal with the crisis by summoning the Estates

1. **absolute** : ruling with unlimited power.
2. **monarchy** : the system in which a country is ruled by a king or queen.
3. **clergy** : religious leaders.
4. **bourgeoisie** : the middle class.
5. **bankruptcy** : the state of being unable to pay your debts.
6. **peasantry** : poor people who did farm work on the piece of land where they lived.
7. **tyranny** : unfair and cruel government.

General – a meeting of representatives from all three social groups. On 17th June, the Third Estate declared that they were the real representatives of France. They formed themselves into the National Assembly. They set about giving the country a new constitution. [1] Louis XVI was forced to recognise the National Assembly, and there was now a period of constitutional monarchy.

The Revolutionary Events

On 14th July, 1789, a huge crowd besieged [2] the Bastille prison in Paris. They entered the prison and killed the soldiers who were defending it. Then they released the prisoners.

The Storming of the Bastille marked the beginning of the French Revolution.

Musée Carnavalet, Paris.

---

1. **constitution** : a set of political principles.
2. **besieged** : attacked.

Capital Execution in Place de la Révolution (1793) by P. A. Demachy
Musée Carnavalet, Paris.

The uprising quickly spread throughout the country. Attacks on property occurred more frequently and many aristocrats, government officials and army officers were hanged. Aristocrats began to flee the country. [1] The National Assembly tried to control the violence. It abolished the exemptions from taxation that had been the cause of so much resentment [2] and in August it issued the Declaration of the Rights of Man.

The biggest threat to the Revolution came from other European monarchies.

The Austrian Emperor and the King of Prussia tried to restore the old system of government in France. The revolutionaries in France responded on 20th April 1792 by declaring war on Austria.

1. **flee the country** : quickly go to another country.
2. **resentment** : hatred.

The war went badly for France at first. Louis XVI was stripped of his title [1] by the Legislative Assembly, and he and his family were imprisoned.

A new government, the National Convention, was established and the Austrians were defeated on 20th September. The Republic was declared on 21st September and Louis XVI was executed [2] in January 1793.

There followed a period of intense violence, particularly in Paris. This was the 'reign of terror', when thousands of aristocrats and other people were put to death on the guillotine.

1 **Answer the following questions.**

    a. Who didn't pay taxes in France before the Revolution?

    b. How was French society divided before the Revolution?

    c. Why were there French soldiers in America during the War of Independence?

    d. What did these French soldiers learn from the Americans?

    e. What was the Estates General?

    f. Why did Louis XVI summon it?

    g. What was the National Assembly?

    h. What happened on July 14, 1789?

    i. How did the National Assembly try to control the violence?

    j. Why did the French revolutionaries declare war on Austria?

    k. When was Louis XVI executed?

    l. What was the 'Reign of Terror'?

---

1. **was stripped of his title** : had his title removed.
2. **executed** : killed.

Before you go on

FCE **1** **Listen to Chapter Seven and choose the best answer (A, B or C).**

1. The revolutionary officials treated Charles roughly because
   A. [ ] he was an aristocrat.
   B. [ ] he was Mr Lorry's friend.
   C. [ ] he lived in England.

2. Lucie knew that Charles had come to France because
   A. [ ] he had told her.
   B. [ ] Mr Lorry had written to her.
   C. [ ] he had written to her.

3. After talking to Mr Lorry, Doctor Manette went immediately to
   A. [ ] London.
   B. [ ] the Bastille where he had been a prisoner.
   C. [ ] the prison where Charles was.

4. The authorities always referred to Charles as
   A. [ ] that Enemy of the people.
   B. [ ] Marquis.
   C. [ ] Evrémonde.

5. What did Doctor Manette succeed in doing?
   A. [ ] He succeeded in convincing the authorities to release Charles from prison.
   B. [ ] He succeeded in convincing the authorities to move Charles to another prison and then to try him before the Tribunal.
   C. [ ] He succeeded in bringing Sydney Carton from London.

6. Mr Lorry's visitor from England was
   A. [ ] Sydney Carton.
   B. [ ] a French spy.
   C. [ ] an English spy.

CHAPTER SEVEN

A Prisoner of the Revolution

Charles Darnay's journey through France was a difficult and dangerous one. He was stopped at every town and his papers were inspected. It soon became known that he was an aristocrat who was journeying to Paris to save the life of an old servant of the family and he was treated roughly [1] by the new revolutionary officials. When he arrived in Paris, he was immediately arrested and thrown into prison.

A few days later, while Mr Lorry was sitting in his office in Paris, there was suddenly a noise outside his office. Two people burst [2] into the room.

'Lucie!' he cried in astonishment. [3] 'And you, Doctor Manette. What are you doing here in Paris?'

'It's Charles,' Lucie explained hurriedly. 'He's here in Paris, in prison.'

---

1. **roughly** : unpleasantly, without consideration.
2. **burst** : entered noisily and quickly.
3. **astonishment** : great surprise.

Then she explained why Darnay had come to France and how he had been arrested.

'It's all in the letter he left for me before he came here,' she explained. 'We must save him!' she cried desperately.

Doctor Manette spoke now. His voice was strong and firm.

'I have great influence here,' he said calmly. 'Everyone knows that I've been a prisoner in the Bastille. They'll listen to me – and I hope they'll let Charles go.'

Doctor Manette left immediately for the prison where Charles was being held. He found the situation there extremely dangerous and chaotic. [1] A lot of prisoners had been murdered by the crowd, and a revolutionary Tribunal [2] had been set up by the authorities for trying those who had survived. This was the time when the

---

1. **chaotic** : completely disorganized.   2. **Tribunal** : a kind of court.

A Tale of Two Cities

guillotine [1] was introduced as the preferred form of execution. Hundreds of people were executed and the dreaded [2] tumbrils [3] carrying aristocrats to their death could be heard on the Paris streets every day. It was a time of fear and terror.

In the days and weeks that followed, Doctor Manette worked hard to save his son-in-law. He went before the Tribunal and explained who he was, and how he had been held in the Bastille for eighteen years without trial. Once the Tribunal knew his history, he was regarded [4] as a friend of the new authorities. They treated him with great respect, but little was done to free Lucie's husband, who was always angrily referred to as 'Evrémonde'.

Months went by and Doctor Manette went to the Tribunal every day to plead [5] his case. Finally, the doctor returned to Mr Lorry's house one night in a mood of great excitement.

'I think I've succeeded,' he told Lucie. 'Charles is going to be moved to another prison tomorrow and then his trial will take place before the Tribunal.' He looked tenderly at her. 'Don't be frightened, my dear. They'll free him, I'm sure of it.'

Outside in the street they could hear the sound of wheels. They both listened, knowing what the noise meant – more tumbrils carrying people to the guillotine.

'I must speak to Mr Lorry,' the doctor said quickly.

Mr Lorry had been sitting in his office with a visitor from England when he heard the voices of Doctor Manette and Lucie. His visitor was Sydney Carton. The lawyer did not want to be seen by the doctor or his daughter because he wanted to keep his presence in Paris a secret for a while. He signalled to the banker to go out to the doctor and Lucie.

---

1. **guillotine** :
2. **dreaded** : fearsome.
3. **tumbrils** : carts.
4. **regarded** : seen.
5. **plead** : present, argue.

Go back to the text

1 **Read Chapter Seven and complete the following sentences.**

a. Revolutionary officials stopped Charles Darnay at every town to
....

b. When Charles Darnay arrived in Paris he was immediately ....
....

c. Lucie and Doctor Manette came to Paris because ....
....

d. The revolutionary Tribunal was set up to try those people who
had not ....

e. The revolutionary Tribunal executed people by means of ....
....

f. The Tribunal regarded Doctor Manette as a friend when they
learned that ....

g. The tumbrils were used to ....
....

h. Sydney Carton signalled to Mr Lorry to leave his office to see
Lucie and Doctor Manette because ....
....

Sentence transformation

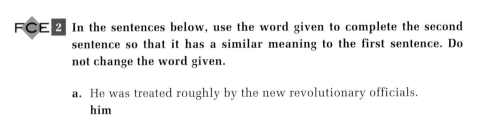

2 **In the sentences below, use the word given to complete the second sentence so that it has a similar meaning to the first sentence. Do not change the word given.**

a. He was treated roughly by the new revolutionary officials.
him
The new revolutionary officials .... roughly.

b. It soon became known that he was an aristocrat.
found
They soon .... an aristocrat.

c. When he arrived in Paris, he was immediately arrested and thrown into prison.

soon

He was arrested .... in Paris.

d. 'We must save him!' she cried desperately.

to

She cried desperately that .... him.

e. 'And you, Doctor Manette, What are you doing here in Paris?'

was

He asked .... there in Paris.

f. 'They'll free him, I'm sure of it.'

would

He was sure that .... him.

g. The lawyer did not want to be seen by the doctor.

see

The lawyer did not want .... him.

The guillotine: a good idea gone bad

 3 Read the article about the guillotine and then choose the correct answer (A, B, C or D) for the questions.

Certainly one of the great ironies of history is that the use of the guillotine for executions was first proposed for humanitarian [1] reasons. During the eighteenth century those who were about to be executed were often tortured in the most horrible ways imaginable, and even after their death their bodies, often cut up into pieces, were displayed before the public: an 'anatomised' body was supposed to act as a deterrent [2] against future crimes. Still, many people at the time realised that the brutality of the punishment helped to increase brutality in society rather than diminish it. In fact a certain Dr Joseph-Ignace Guillotin (1738-1814), a physician [3] elected to the French National Assembly in 1789, tried to stop the barbarous means of execution of his time; he promoted a law which established that a condemned person was to be beheaded

---

1. **humanitarian** : reducing suffering.
2. **deterrent** : threat.
3. **physician** : doctor.

without torture; in addition his law stated that the body of the victim was to be returned to the family and not exposed in public.

This then is why that monstrous [1] machinery used for cutting off human heads now bears his name; he was not, though, its inventor. Similar machines had been used in Europe for centuries, and the machine actually put in use during the French Revolution was built using the plans of Dr Antoine Louis of the Académie Chirugical. Indeed, the first head-cutting machines were referred to as 'Louisons' and not 'guillotines'.

The actual construction of the first guillotine was entrusted to a German harpsichord [2] maker named Tobias Schmidt, and the improvement on the blade [3] itself, which made it slanted and not straight, was the idea of a famous mechanical tinker [4] of the time and one of the machine's most illustrious victims, Louis XVI himself.

After testing prototypes on sheep, calves and cadavers, the guillotine, or the 'razor of the French Revolution' as it was nicknamed, was ready for use, and the rest is, as they say, history. Thousands and thousands were placed face down on the bench with their head between two uprights; then the 40-kilo blade would fall a distance of 2.3 metres at 7 metres a second, hitting the neck with a force of 400 kilos per square inch. This whole process took less than half a second.

Obviously the massive use of the guillotine eliminated any humanitarian aspect it might have had at the beginning; and some have even claimed that victims of the guillotine did not lose consciousness completely until thirty seconds after their heads were cut off. A truly terrifying thought! Fortunately, this horrible instrument is no longer in official use in France: the last public execution having occurred in 1939, and the last official execution in 1977.

1. **monstrous** : very cruel.
2. **harpsichord** : a musical instrument similar to a small piano.
3. **blade** :
4. **tinker** : a person who worked with mechanical things.

1. The story of the guillotine is ironic because

A. ☐ it was not actually invented by Dr Joesph-Ignace Guillotin.

B. ☐ Louis XVI helped to improve its construction.

C. ☐ it was proposed for use to eliminate barbarous torture but then it became an instrument of terror.

D. ☐ it was known as the 'razor' of the French Revolution.

2. Why did Dr Guillotin propose the use of the guillotine for executions?

    A. ☐ He wished to make executions more humane and eliminate the barbarous methods in use at the time.

    B. ☐ He wished to construct a machine that could kill as many people as possible in the shortest period of time.

    C. ☐ He wished to frighten people so that they would not commit crimes.

    D. ☐ He wished to make it easier to cut up the bodies of the victims.

3. Why is the head-cutting machine used during the French Revolution called a 'guillotine'?

    A. ☐ Because a man named Dr Guillotin built the first one in history.

    B. ☐ Because a man named Dr Guillotin promoted a law which established its use for executions.

    C. ☐ Because a man named Dr Guillotin designed the one used during the French Revolution.

    D. ☐ Because a man named Dr Guillotin fought against the use of this barbarous machine.

4. Who constructed the first guillotine?

    A. ☐ Dr Guillotin

    B. ☐ Dr Louis

    C. ☐ Mr Schmidt

    D. ☐ Louis XVI

5. Why might the guillotine not have been a humane way of executing someone?

    A. ☐ The beheaded person might not have lost consciousness until thirty seconds after his head was cut off.

    B. ☐ The huge blade fell at a frightening speed.

    C. ☐ The victim had to lie face down on a bench.

    D. ☐ The victim was sure that he would die.

CHAPTER EIGHT

Joy and Despair

The prisoner Evrémonde was summoned to appear before the Tribunal. Most of the prisoners who had been tried there were already dead, and the Tribunal was feared because of its passion for the death sentence. Charles Darnay looked around him in confusion when he entered the court. The judges sat on a bench at one end of the hall and the rest of the space was taken up by a crowd of jeering, [1] laughing people who watched the evidence being given. The crowd commented loudly on everything that was said. They cheered when they heard something they liked and hissed [2] when they heard something they did not like.

The crowd knew the name of Evrémonde and they hissed at the prisoner when he came forward. There were cries of 'Death to the enemy of the Republic!' and 'Take off his head!' Then the evidence began.

The prisoner admitted who he was. He said that he had always

---

1. **jeering** : mocking, ridiculing.
2. **hissed** : made a noise indicating their disapproval.

A Tale of Two Cities

been opposed to the cruelties of the old system. He said that he had not wanted to benefit from his properties in France after the death of his uncle the Marquis. He had been working for a living in England. He gave the names of two witnesses who would support what he said: Gabelle and Alexandre Manette.

The crowd in the court cheered at the name of Doctor Manette. His story was a famous one and he was a hero in their eyes. When the prisoner added that he was married to Doctor Manette's daughter, the attitude of the crowd softened towards him.

Gabelle was called to give evidence and he confirmed what the prisoner had said about his inheritance. Evrémonde had never benefited from his land or property in France. Evrémonde had

Joy and Despair

come back to France after he, Gabelle, had written to him asking for help. Again the crowd cheered when they heard this evidence.

Now it was Doctor Manette's turn to speak. He said that the prisoner had always been his friend. The prisoner lived in England, but was not a friend of the aristocratic regime [1] there – he had even been tried for treason by the English. The doctor spoke calmly and clearly and the crowd was convinced by what he told the court. They began to shout 'Free the prisoner!' and 'Let him go!'

The judges were also convinced by the evidence of Doctor Manette. They gave their verdict: ACQUITTED.

The prisoner Evrémonde was carried out of the court by the joyful crowd who had been calling for his death only a short while

1. **regime** : system of government.

before. He was embraced and cheered and then placed in a chair and paraded [1] in the streets. The excited crowd escorted [2] him to Doctor Manette's house. Mr Lorry was there to welcome him, as was Miss Pross, who had accompanied them to Paris, and Jerry Cruncher. Lucie and the doctor were waiting for him inside the house.

Darnay greeted Mr Lorry and Miss Pross hurriedly and then went into the house to join his wife. He embraced her and the tears fell from Lucie's face. Darnay held his wife for a few minutes and then he said:

'We must speak to your father, my dear. No other man in France could have done what he did. No other man could have saved me as he did.'

The doctor was proud of what he had done. He had promised Lucie that he would save her husband and he had succeeded. There was no trace of weakness in the old man's features [3] now. He was calm and confident.

Soon afterwards Mr Lorry returned to his office at Tellson's Bank and Jerry and Miss Pross went out to do some shopping for the family. Doctor Manette, Darnay and Lucie sat quietly together talking over everything that had happened. They had not been talking for very long when they heard footsteps in the street outside. Lucie went very pale.

'Soldiers!' she cried. 'Hide Charles, Father, hide him!'

'Be quiet, Lucie,' her father replied. 'Charles is safe – I have saved him. We have nothing to fear.'

The doctor went to the door to see what was happening. Four men armed with pistols pushed past him into the house.

'Where is Evrémonde, also called Darnay?' one of them asked roughly.

---

1. **paraded** : marched.
2. **escorted** : accompanied.
3. **features** : face.

Joy and Despair

Darnay stood up.

'I am Evrémonde,' he told the man quietly. 'What do you want?'

'You're under arrest,' the man told him. 'You must come with us.'

'Tell me why I'm under arrest,' Darnay asked quietly.

'You'll know soon enough,' one of the men replied. 'Now you must come with us.'

Doctor Manette stepped forward and asked the men, 'Do you know who I am?'

'We know you, Doctor Manette,' the men said respectfully.

'Then tell me why he is under arrest,' the doctor asked.

'He has been accused by Citizen Defarge and Madame Defarge,' the man said. 'And by one other person as well.'

'Who?' asked the doctor. 'Who is the third person?'

The men looked at Doctor Manette in surprise. For a moment there was an awkward silence.

'You don't know who it was?' one of them asked.

'No, I don't,' the doctor replied.

The other man shrugged and told him:

'You will know tomorrow.'

The soldiers took Darnay into custody [1] and marched him off to prison. His new trial was set for the following day.

---

1. **custody** : prison.

Go back to the text

1 **Answer the following questions.**

    a. Why does the Tribunal refer to Charles as Evrémonde?

    b. How does the crowd react during the trial?

    c. How does Gabelle help Charles during the trial?

    d. Why does Charles' marriage to Lucie help him during the trial?

    e. How does Alexandre Manette prove that Charles is not a friend of the English nobles?

    f. What was the court's verdict?

    g. Why did Alexandre Manette feel proud after the trial?

    h. Who were Charles's accusers the second time that he was arrested?

The fickle crowd

2 **'Mob' means 'a wild and uncontrollable crowd', and it comes from the Latin 'mobile vulgus' which can be translated as 'the fickle crowd'. Look up the word 'fickle' in your dictionary and say why or why not it describes the crowd attending the trial of Charles Darnay.**

Past Perfect Continuous or Past Continuous?

'He had been working for a living in England.'

The Past Perfect Continuous is formed in this way.

Subject + **had been** + ing-form of verb
   He   ***had been***   ***waiting*** *for an hour.*

The Past Perfect Continuous is the past of the Present Perfect Continuous.

The Present Perfect Continuous has two basic uses in English.
The first is to express the duration of an event that began in the past
and continues up to the present.

I have been waiting for an hour. = He began waiting an hour ago, and
he is still waiting.
With the Past Perfect Continuous the point of reference instead of
being the present is a point of time in the past.
When I arrived at ten o'clock yesterday, he **had been waiting** *for me
for an hour.*
In this sentence the point of reference is 'ten o'clock yesterday'.

The Present Perfect Continuous has another common use similar to
duration: it describes an action which began in the past and which
has recently stopped.
They **have been running**. *Look they are out of breath.*
This is not the same as
They **are running**.

In the same way sentences in the Past Perfect Continuous are not the
same as sentences in the Past Continuous.
When I arrived I could see that they **had been running**: *they were out
of breath.* (They were not running when I saw them.)
They **were running** *when I saw them.*

3 **Put the verbs in brackets in the Past Perfect Continuous or the Past
Continuous according to the context.**

Example: When I entered the classroom all the students were writing.
They (*take*) ...were taking... a test.

When I saw Herbert at the restaurant his hair had blue spots
all over it. He (*paint*) ..had been painting.. his house.

a. I (*drive*) .... along the motorway, when suddenly
the car stopped.

b. They (*dance*) .... for three hours when they
suddenly realised that their friends had gone.

c. Jack and I were sitting on a bench, relaxing. He told me that he was really tired because he (*work*) .... hard that week.

d. When I came into the room Charles and Sydney were shouting. They (*argue*) .... about Lucie.

e. We (*swim*) .... for half an hour, when Helen saw a shark.

f. Susan was covered with mud from head to toe. She (*play*) .... football in the rain.

g. I looked out of the window and saw some children on the playing field. They (*play*) .... football.

h. Everybody was standing around with an innocent look on their face, but I could smell smoke so I knew that they (*smoke*) ....

Summing it all up

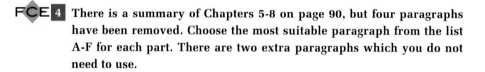 **There is a summary of Chapters 5-8 on page 90, but four paragraphs have been removed. Choose the most suitable paragraph from the list A-F for each part. There are two extra paragraphs which you do not need to use.**

A. So, he then went to the prison. It was a very dangerous period and many people had already been condemned by the revolutionary Tribunal. Fortunately, Doctor Manette was right though: the authorities considered him as a kind of hero, and in the end they moved Charles to another prison and his trial was scheduled.

B. Doctor Manette, Lucie and Charles all returned happily to Doctor Manette's house. Doctor Manette was particularly proud and happy because he had promised Lucie that he would save Charles and he did. But not too much later there was a knock at the door. Doctor Manette opened the door and there were some soldiers who announced that Evrémonde was under arrest. They said that he was accused by Citizen Defarge, Madame Defarge and a third person.

C. It was then that Sydney Carton had an idea how to save Charles. He went to Doctor Manette and told him to ask the judges if they were sure Charles was really the right person, and if they did not think that Charles looked a great deal like Sydney Carton. The judges looked at the two men, and indeed they did look like twins. So, they acquitted Charles and he left together with Lucie and Doctor Manette to celebrate their great victory.

D. Once the old prison had been captured Monsieur Defarge looked for the cell where Doctor Manette had been imprisoned for so many years. Finally he found a cell with the initials 'A. M.' on the wall. Then he searched an old fireplace and found some papers. These papers would later almost mean Charles Darnay's death. At the moment though Charles Darnay was still in London, but he had just received a letter from his former servant Gabelle. Gabelle was in prison and asked Charles for help. Charles decided to return to France to help him.

E. Just before the wedding, Charles spoke to Doctor Manette in private; he told him his real name; and Doctor Manette appeared to be very upset by what Charles told him. However, at the wedding ceremony Doctor Manette did his best to be cheerful. After the wedding Charles and Lucie went away on their honeymoon, leaving her father behind. He seemed to be sad at first, and then he became totally lost in his thoughts of his prison years and began making shoes. Fortunately, after ten days, he came to himself again.

F. After the trial, Charles Darnay settled in England and became a French teacher. He, along with Mr Lorry and Sydney Carton, became friends with Doctor Manette and his daughter. Eventually, Charles fell in love with Lucie, and he told her father of his intentions. He also told her father that he wanted to reveal his real name. Doctor Manette looked frightened at this and told him to wait till the wedding day. Sydney Carton also told Lucie that he was in love with her, but he realised that he was not good enough to marry her; still, he promised that if she or her family ever needed him, he would be glad to do anything for them.

1.

Six years later in July of 1789, Lucie and Charles were still happily married and they had a little girl named Lucie. Their happy world, though, was about to be turned upside down by the revolution that was about to begin in France. Mr Lorry felt the first effects of the revolution because his French clients wanted to send their valuables and money to England. In Paris Doctor Manette's former servant, Monsieur Defarge, was about to take part in the event that signalled the actual beginning of the French Revolution: the storming of the Bastille!

2.

Soon after his arrival in France, the authorities discovered that he was really a French aristocrat named Evrémonde and he was thrown in prison. Lucie and her father immediately came to Paris when they heard about Charles. They went immediately to the office of Mr Lorry. Doctor Manette explained to Mr Lorry that the fact that he had been a prisoner in the Bastille would help him to free Charles.

3.

Finally the trial began, and the Tribunal called him 'Evrémonde' and the crowd hissed and booed [1] him. It did not look good until Gabelle and Doctor Manette began to testify on his behalf. Doctor Manette was then a kind of hero of the revolution so when he said that Charles had always been his friend and that he was an enemy of the aristocratic regime in England, the crowd began to shout, 'Free the prisoner!' In the end Charles was acquitted.

4.

---

1.   **booed** : showed contempt by shouting "boo".

Before you go on

FCE **1** **Read the text below and decide which answer A, B, C or D best fits each space. There is an example at the beginning.**

Jerry and Miss Pross did not know that Charles Darnay had been re-arrested by the court. They were walking through the streets together, (**0**).......A....... what they should buy at the market. Miss Pross (**1**)................. her shopping bag with her and looked cheerfully into the shop windows as they went along.
They went into a wine shop and placed their order. (**2**)................. they waited, Miss Pross looked around the shop (**3**)................. the other customers. Suddenly, she (**4**)................. a scream and clapped her hands together.
'Solomon!' she cried, rushing up to a man who was standing (**5**)................. himself in the shop. 'Solomon, my own brother!'
'What's the matter?' the man asked. Then he looked at her and went very pale. 'Don't (**6**)................. me Solomon,' he whispered fiercely. 'Do you want to be the death of me?'
'Brother!' cried Miss Pross again.
The man gave her a frightened(**7**)................. and hurried out of the shop. He made a sign to Miss Pross to (**8**)................. him into the street.
'What do you want?' he (**9**)................. her coldly, once they were outside the shop.
'How can you talk to me like that?' Miss Pross exclaimed sadly.
'Haven't you got any (**10**)................. for me at all, Solomon?'
The man hastily kissed her.
'Now go away,' he said roughly. 'I'm an official here and you're (**11**)................. me in great danger. If people knew that we were brother and sister –!'
Jerry had been silent up to now, but he had been (**12**)................. the man very carefully.
'What's your real name?' he asked the man thoughtfully. 'Is it John or

is it Solomon? She calls you Solomon – but I knew you
(**13**)................. John. And your second name wasn't Pross when you
were in England!'
'What do you (**14**).................?'
'I (**15**)................. you, you see,' Jerry said slowly. 'You were a
witness at an Old Bailey trial.

0.	**A.** planning	**B.** plotting	**C.** inventing	**D.** developing
1.	**A.** held	**B.** transported	**C.** carried	**D.** fetched
2.	**A.** When	**B.** Like	**C.** Meantime	**D.** As
3.	**A.** at	**B.** to	**C.** for	**D.** in
4.	**A.** took	**B.** gave	**C.** threw	**D.** pronounced
5.	**A.** by	**B.** with	**C.** from	**D.** to
6.	**A.** name	**B.** tell	**C.** call	**D.** cry
7.	**A.** expression	**B.** face	**C.** eye	**D.** look
8.	**A.** pursue	**B.** hunt	**C.** chase	**D.** follow
9.	**A.** asked	**B.** requested	**C.** enquired	**D.** demanded
10.	**A.** emotion	**B.** feelings	**C.** loves	**D.** feeling
11.	**A.** putting	**B.** making	**C.** doing	**D.** imposing
12.	**A.** read	**B.** inspecting	**C.** checking	**D.** studying
13.	**A.** for	**B.** like	**C.** as	**D.** by
14.	**A.** intend	**B.** mean	**C.** signify	**D.** say
15.	**A.** remember	**B.** repeal	**C.** remind	**D.** recollect

 Now listen to the recording and check your answers.

CHAPTER NINE

Sydney Carton Plays Cards

Jerry and Miss Pross did not know that Charles Darnay had been re-arrested by the court. They were walking through the streets together, planning what they should buy at the market. Miss Pross carried her shopping bag with her and looked cheerfully into the shop windows as they went along.

They went into a wine shop and placed their order. As they waited, Miss Pross looked around the shop at the other customers. Suddenly, she gave a scream and clapped her hands together. [1]

'Solomon!' she cried, rushing up to a man who was standing by himself in the shop. 'Solomon, my own brother!'

'What's the matter?' the man asked. Then he looked at her and went very pale. 'Don't call me Solomon,' he whispered fiercely. [2] 'Do you want to be the death of me?'

---

1. **clapped her hands together** : hit her hands together to show happiness.
2. **fiercely** : angrily and aggressively.

'Brother!' cried Miss Pross again.

The man gave her a frightened look and hurried out of the shop. He made a sign to Miss Pross to follow him into the street.

'What do you want?' he asked her coldly, once they were outside the shop.

'How can you talk to me like that?' Miss Pross exclaimed sadly. 'Haven't you got any feelings for me at all, Solomon?'

The man hastily [1] kissed her.

'Now go away,' he said roughly. 'I'm an official here and you're putting me in great danger. If people knew that we were brother and sister –!'

Jerry had been silent up to now, but he had been studying [2] the man very carefully.

'What's your real name?' he asked the man thoughtfully. 'Is it John or is it Solomon? She calls you Solomon – but I knew you as John. And your second name wasn't Pross when you were in England!'

'What do you mean?'

'I remember you, you see,' Jerry said slowly. 'You were a witness at an Old Bailey trial. You were a government spy and you gave evidence against the prisoner. You were called John something. I remember the John part all right, but I don't remember the rest. What was it?'

'Barsad,' a voice uttered [3] quietly.

'That's the name!' Jerry shouted excitedly. He turned to see who had spoken and found himself facing Sydney Carton.

'Don't be frightened, Miss Pross,' Carton said quietly. 'I arrived today. I'm staying at Mr Lorry's.' **E-3** END

---

1. **hastily** : quickly.
2. **studying** : observing.
3. **uttered** : spoke.

A Tale of Two Cities

The young lawyer looked at Miss Pross' brother with anger and contempt.

'I'm sorry about your brother, though. He's what they call a sheep of the prisons.'[1]

The man turned even paler when he heard this accusation. He looked at Sydney Carton in great fear. Carton looked back at him quietly and then went on.

'I saw you coming out of the prison, you know. I remembered you very well from the treason trial at the Old Bailey, Mr Barsad. It wasn't difficult for me to guess what you were doing here in Paris. And it gave me an idea, you see.'

'What idea?' the man asked nervously. 'What are you talking about?'

'It would be difficult to discuss my idea here, among all this crowd,' Carton replied with a smile. 'Why don't we go to Tellson's Bank? We can talk quietly there.'

'Why should I go with you?' the man asked.

'I can't say why,' Carton replied smoothly.

'You mean you won't say why!' the man said.

Sydney Carton smiled again.

'Precisely. You understand me very well.'

Sydney Carton and John Barsad, or Solomon Pross, were soon sitting in Tellson's Bank talking to Mr Lorry. Carton explained very quickly who the man was and Mr Lorry remembered him from the Old Bailey trial. The banker looked in disgust at Miss Pross' brother. Then Carton told Mr Lorry about Charles Darnay having been arrested again.

'I don't know if Doctor Manette will be able to save him this time,' Carton said. 'These are desperate times, Mr Lorry, and I

---

1. **sheep of the prisons** : a term used during the French Revolution to describe an informer.

Sydney Carton Plays Cards

think the doctor's influence with the court is on the wane. [1] Yes, desperate times indeed,' he said thoughtfully. 'And desperate times call for a desperate game. My game is to win a friend inside the prison. You, Mr Barsad!' he announced firmly.

'You'll need good cards to win that game,' the spy said coldly.

'In a moment I'll show you my cards,' Carton said grimly. 'But first, if you don't mind, Mr Lorry, some brandy!'

Mr Lorry brought over a bottle of brandy and placed it in front of Sydney Carton. The lawyer quickly drank two full glasses of it and then turned back to the spy.

'You're an informer,' he said calmly. 'You work for the French authorities in the prison. Your job is to listen to the prisoners and to report what they say. But you used to be a spy for the British government, didn't you? That's my first card, Mr Barsad – your career in London. I wonder what the French authorities would say if they knew that? Would they think you were still a spy for the British government? Would they see you as a traitor?' [2]

He paused to take another glass of brandy.

'Now look at your cards, Mr Barsad,' he advised pleasantly. 'What have you got?'

The spy was silent for a moment. He was thinking hard. Everything that the lawyer had told him was true. He had indeed been a spy for the British government. He had lost that job because it was soon discovered that the evidence he gave at trials – like the trial of Charles Darnay at the Old Bailey – was unreliable. He had then come to France, where he had worked for the government before the Revolution. After the Revolution he had changed sides and now worked for the very people he had spied on before! He was in a dangerous position and he knew it.

1. **on the wane** : becoming weaker.
2. **traitor** : a person who betrays their country.

A Tale of Two Cities

'You don't seem to like your cards,' Carton commented wryly. [1] 'Are you going to play, my friend?'

Miss Pross' brother sighed deeply. He realised that he was beaten. [2]

'You told me you had an idea, Mr Carton,' he said wearily. 'I'd like to hear it. But I warn you, you can't ask too much of me. Don't ask me to do anything dangerous.'

Sydney Carton smiled at him.

'I'm not asking much,' he told him. 'You're one of the prison gaolers, aren't you?'

'Escape is impossible!' the spy hurriedly interrupted. 'I won't have anything to do with it – it's too dangerous.'

'I have not said anything about an escape,' the lawyer reminded him softly. 'But there is something you can do for me. We'll discuss it in private, if you don't mind.'

He stood up and went into another room and John Barsad followed him. Sydney Carton closed the door carefully and Mr Lorry could hear them talking earnestly [3] in low voices. Their discussion went on for a long time.

---

1. **wryly** : with an ironic tone.
2. **beaten** : defeated.
3. **earnestly** : very seriously.

Go back to the text

1 **Say whether the following statements are True (T) or False (F), and then correct the false ones.**

		T	F
a.	Miss Pross went to the wine shop to meet her brother.	☐	☐
b.	Solomon was not very happy to see his sister.	☐	☐
c.	Jerry had already seen Solomon before in England.	☐	☐
d.	Solomon was a spy for the government in England before he came to France.	☐	☐
e.	Sydney Carton did not understand what Solomon was doing in Paris.	☐	☐
f.	Solomon used the name John Barsad in England.	☐	☐
g.	Sydney Carton does not think that Doctor Manette will be able to save Charles a second time.	☐	☐
h.	John Barsad has a friend who is an informer in the prison.	☐	☐
i.	John Barsad agrees to Sydney Carton's plan because he is worried about Charles.	☐	☐
j.	Sydney Carton wants John Barsad to help Charles escape from prison.	☐	☐

Miss Pross' brother is John Barsad. What a coincidence!

2 **Although Charles Dickens is considered one of the greatest writers of English literature, some have criticised him for his melodramatic style: he often uses fantastic coincidences in his novels which most modern writers would never use. *A Tale of Two Cities* is no exception. Here are two coincidences we have seen so far in the book. Explain why they are coincidences.**

- Mr Lorry travelled with Charles Darnay on the same boat back from France.

- Miss Pross' brother is John Barsad.

The best of the lot

 3 You have read *A Tale of Two Cities*, and your friend has suggested that you watch the 1980 film version of the novel. You, however, think that the 1935 film version of the film is the best choice.
Write a short proposal of between 120 and 180 words supporting your choice. You can use the following information.

- Sydney Carton played by Ronald Colman, one of the great actors in history of Hollywood.

- Seven film versions of this film, first in 1911, last in 1980, but this version considered the best.

- His final lines, 'It is a far, far better thing that I do, than I have ever done...' one of the most famous lines from any film in history.

- Actress Blanche Yurka wonderfully evil as the ruthless [1] Madame Defarge.

- Basil Rathbone, who gives a great performance as the evil Marquis Evrémonde, later became famous for his interpretation of Sherlock Holmes.

- Val Lewton and Jacques Tourneur, who directed the scenes of the storming of the Bastille worked together years later on such horror classics as *Cat People* and *I Walked with a Zombie*.

- Producer of film, David O Selznick later the producer of *Gone With the Wind*.

- Two Oscar nominations.

- More than 15,000 extras used in the mob scenes.

THE REVIEWS

David Kehr ☆ ☆ ☆ *(out of four)*
This MGM version of the Dickens novel is as spectacular as these things go.

---

1.   **ruthless** : cruel.

Sam Ashby ☆ ☆ ☆ ☆
This superb, lavish [1] production features an MGM stock company playing every small role to perfection, and Colman gives one of the best performances of his life.

Pauline Kael ☆ ☆ ☆
As Madame Defarge, Blanche Yurka dominates the film; a menace in the grand manner, she knits like a house afire and takes the Bastille practically single-handed.

Leonard Matlin ☆ ☆ ☆ ☆
Dickens's panorama [2] of the 1780 French Revolution becomes an MGM blockbuster... Tremendous cast in a truly lavish production.

You can begin like this:
I realise that nowadays my friends are used to seeing films with incredible special effects and amazing colours, but I think this black and white film from 1935 will surprise them...

Before you go on

1 **The Third Man**
Whom do you think the 'third' accuser is?

---

1. **lavish** : expensive.
2. **panorama** : view.

CHAPTER TEN

Secrets from the Past

Darnay's second trial began like the first one. There was the same riotous [1] crowd commenting on the prisoners and calling out insults to the defendant. There was the same dreaded Tribunal. The proceedings [2] started when the President asked who had accused the prisoner.

'There are three accusers,' the court official announced. 'Defarge, the wine shopkeeper, Madame Defarge – and Doctor Manette.'

There was a gasp of astonishment from the crowd when they heard Doctor Manette named as an accuser. Everybody remembered that he had spoken in Evrémonde's favour at the previous trial. Doctor Manette rose hurriedly to his feet to protest at the use of his name.

'This is outrageous!' [3] he told the court. 'You know that the prisoner is my son-in-law. I have not accused him of anything –

---

1. **riotous** : noisy and uncontrolled.
2. **proceedings** : steps in a law case.
3. **outrageous** : shocking and unacceptable.

and I never would!'

'Be silent,' the President said. 'Listen to the evidence.'

Defarge was called to speak. He confirmed that he had taken part in the attack on the Bastille at the beginning of the Revolution.

'What did you do after the prison was taken?' he was asked.

'I knew that Doctor Manette had been imprisoned in the Bastille,' Defarge explained. 'I had been his servant before he was imprisoned, and I had always felt his sufferings deeply. I went to his old cell and I searched it. I found a paper written by the Doctor – it was hidden in the chimney.'

Doctor Manette turned very pale when he heard this evidence. He began to shake and a confused expression came into his eyes. His former strength and confidence deserted [1] him and he looked old, weak and defenceless. He looked wildly about the court, and then staggered [2] back to his seat.

The President took the paper and read its contents to the court:

I, Alexandre Manette, a doctor, am writing this in the hope that someone will read it after my death. I have been imprisoned here without trial and I wish to explain what happened to me.

One night I was out walking when two men approached me. They asked if I was Doctor Manette. When I told them that I was, they asked me to go with them to treat [3] a sick woman. They had a carriage waiting. The men did not give me their names, but I was sure that they came from a noble family because of the way that they were dressed and the way that they spoke.

I went with them. The carriage took us to an old house that looked as if it had been abandoned. They took me upstairs to see my

---

1. **deserted** : left.
2. **staggered** : walked with difficulty.
3. **treat** : give medical attention to.

patient. She was a very beautiful, young, peasant woman and she was very sick indeed. I did what I could to make her last hours comfortable. She was very distressed [1] and I understood that some terrible unhappiness had recently occurred. She kept repeating the words, 'My husband, my father and my brother!'

The two men, who I was sure were brothers, looked on as I attended to [2] the girl. Their attitude towards her was a cruel one. They seemed bored by her sufferings. At last the poor girl was quiet and the brothers approached the bed.

'There is another patient,' one of them said. 'Come with me, Doctor.'

They led me to a different room where a young man was lying on the floor. He had a terrible sword wound and it was clear that he could not live long. The young man looked over my shoulder at the two brothers and began to speak furiously and defiantly. [3]

'These nobles are very proud,' he said. 'They thought they could take my sister for their pleasure. But she wouldn't listen to them, Doctor. She had a husband whom she loved. So they took her husband and they made him work day and night without food or sleep. Still he would not agree to what they wanted. They kept him working day and night until he died from exhaustion. [4] Then they seized my sister and carried her away with them. When my father heard what they had done, it broke his heart and he died. I was afraid for my younger sister, so I took her and hid her with some relatives in the country. Then I followed the brothers here to Paris. I climbed into this house to try to save my older sister — but it was too late. I attacked them, but they defended themselves.'

---

1. **distressed** : upset, worried.
2. **attended to** : looked after.
3. **defiantly** : boldly, bravely.
4. **exhaustion** : extreme tiredness.

A Tale of Two Cities

The boy died soon afterwards and his poor sister died later that night. The brothers seemed pleased at the news of her death. They offered me money for my services, but I refused to take it. I was horrified at what they had done to this innocent family.

When I reached home, I wrote a full account [1] of what had happened and sent it to the government minister. I knew that a terrible crime had been committed by these brothers and I felt it was my duty to tell the authorities.

The next day I had a visitor. It was the Marquis St. Evrémonde's wife. She came to see me with her little boy, Charles. She had discovered the whole story and she had come to me because she wanted to help the family that her husband and his twin brother had destroyed. She wanted to find the remaining sister and help her. She was a good woman, and she said something that I've always remembered. When she was saying goodbye, she looked down at her little son and told me:

'I must find that sister. I feel that if I do not try to put things right, my little son may suffer for the wickedness of his father and his uncle.'

A few days later a man in black called at my house. He said there was an urgent case for me and that he had a carriage waiting. I agreed to go at once.

As soon as I entered the carriage someone grabbed hold of me and I could not move. The carriage stopped in front of two men who were standing in the street. I recognised the two brothers immediately. One of them stepped forward with a sneer [2] and threw the letter I had written to the authorities into the carriage. Then he gave a signal and the carriage drove away.

The carriage brought me here to the Bastille and I have remained

---

1. **account** : description.   2. **sneer** : an unpleasant look.

here ever since. I have never been tried for any offence. I understand now that the Marquis St. Evrémonde and his brother had used their aristocratic privilege to have me imprisoned with a lettre de cachet.

My life has been destroyed by the Evrémonde family and their wickedness. I denounce them and their descendants – there can be no forgiveness for any of them!

There was a stunned [1] silence in the court after the reading of Doctor Manette's statement. Then the crowd began to shout angrily.

'No forgiveness for any of them! No forgiveness for any of them!'

Soon everyone in the court was crying the same thing. The President looked at the shouting crowd before he pronounced the Tribunal's verdict on the prisoner: GUILTY – THE GUILLOTINE.

Lucie fell when she heard the verdict of death on her husband. But a moment later, determined to be strong for his sake, [2] she stood up again.

'Let me touch him, I beg you, good citizens,' she said to the gaolers [3] who surrounded Charles Darnay. It happened that Barsad was standing near the prisoner.

'Let her come close,' he told the gaolers. 'Let her come for a moment.'

Darnay leaned over the dock to take her in his arms.

'Farewell, [4] my dear,' he whispered.

Doctor Manette came forward to the dock, and Darnay could see that the old man felt responsible for the disaster that had struck.

'It's not your fault,' Darnay said to him. 'Now I know what terrible sufferings you had in the past. I know how difficult it must

---

1. **stunned** : shocked.
2. **sake** : benefit.
3. **gaolers** : prison guards.
4. **farewell** : goodbye.

A Tale of Two Cities

have been for you to agree to our marriage – but I thank you for your strength in putting Lucie's happiness first.'

The gaolers now took Charles Darnay away. Sydney Carton stepped forward and helped Lucie out of the court.

Later that day Doctor Manette, Sydney Carton and Mr Lorry were talking over what could be done.

'You had great influence with the court, Doctor Manette,' Sydney Carton said. 'Perhaps they would listen to you again.'

'I'll try, of course I'll try everything I can,' the doctor said. His voice trembled with age and grief. [1] After a few minutes he left the room to go and comfort his daughter.

Mr Lorry approached Sydney Carton, and the two men talked quietly together.

'I have no hope,' Mr Lorry said desperately.

'Nor have I,' the lawyer replied. 'Nor have I.'

Carton said quietly, 'Listen to me carefully. Paris is not safe for Lucie now – you must get her away from here tomorrow afternoon. Have a carriage ready outside the house. Wait for me inside the carriage with Lucie, her child and Doctor Manette. As soon as I climb in, give the order to leave. Will you do that, exactly as I've told you?'

Mr Lorry gave the lawyer a strange look, and then he replied.

'I'll have the carriage ready tomorrow afternoon,' he promised.

When Sydney Carton walked away from the house later that day, he was deep in thought. He headed for the Saint Antoine district of the city. He went into Defarge's wine shop and sat down at a table.

Madame Defarge looked curiously at him, and went to take his order. He spoke to her in French, but he made sure that he spoke

---

1. **grief** : sadness.

bad French.

'Are you English?' Madame Defarge asked.

'Yes, Madame, I am English,' he replied.

A few minutes later Defarge brought his wine to him. He, too, looked attentively at the Englishman, and then went back to his wife.

'Certainly, a little like him,' he said softly to her.

Another customer came into the shop and began to talk excitedly to Defarge and his wife. Carton listened to their talk.

'This doctor is not loyal to the Republic,' Madame Defarge said angrily. 'I watched him today and I saw that.'

'You saw his daughter as well,' Defarge reminded her. 'Both she and the old man are suffering terribly.'

'The daughter!' Madame Defarge cried. 'If I had my way –'

'And I say enough,' Defarge told her. 'Evrémonde will die. That must be enough.'

'I have a special reason for hating the Evrémondes,' Madame Defarge said. 'My husband knows that.'

'It's true,' Defarge agreed.

'When you found that paper of the doctor's hidden at the Bastille, you brought it here, remember?' Madame Defarge went on excitedly. 'We read it together. And then I told you about myself. That girl who was killed by the Evrémonde brothers was my own sister!'

'It's true,' Defarge admitted.

'Then don't tell me it's enough!' cried Madame Defarge with hatred. 'The Evrémonde family destroyed my family – and now it's my turn!'

Go back to the text

FCE 1 **Choose the correct answer (A, B, C or D).**

1. Everybody in the court was shocked when they heard that Doctor Manette was one of the accusers because
   A. ☐ he was so old.
   B. ☐ he had defended Charles during the first trial.
   C. ☐ he had been in prison and should have hated the nobility.
   D. ☐ they thought that he had died in the Bastille.

2. Defarge was so interested in Doctor Manette because
   A. ☐ he thought Doctor Manette was a great man.
   B. ☐ Doctor Manette had saved his sister's life before being thrown in prison.
   C. ☐ he had been Doctor Manette's servant.
   D. ☐ Madame Manette had been Doctor Manette's servant.

3. What had Defarge found in Doctor Manette's prison cell?
   A. ☐ a paper containing Doctor Manette's story of why he was in prison
   B. ☐ Doctor Manette's written accusations against Charles Darnay and the bad things that Charles had done against him
   C. ☐ Doctor Manette's written descriptions of his life as a doctor
   D. ☐ Doctor Manette's letter to Lucie

4. Who took Doctor Manette to the dying peasant girl?
   A. ☐ her husband and brother
   B. ☐ her father
   C. ☐ Charles Darnay's father and uncle
   D. ☐ Charles Darnay's twin brother

5. Who was the other patient?

   A. ☐ Charles Darnay's brother

   B. ☐ Doctor Manette's uncle

   C. ☐ Monsieur Defarge's brother

   D. ☐ Madame Defarge's brother

6. To whom did Doctor Manette write about the death of the peasant girl?

   A. ☐ the government

   B. ☐ the Tribunal

   C. ☐ the Marquis St. Evrémonde's wife

   D. ☐ Charles Darnay

7. Charles's mother came to see Doctor Manette because

   A. ☐ she had received his letter.

   B. ☐ she felt that her little boy would somehow suffer for the terrible things that his father had done.

   C. ☐ she was worried about what would happen to her husband if the government learned about his crime.

   D. ☐ she was worried about Doctor Manette.

8. Why did Doctor Manette actually denounce Charles Darnay?

   A. ☐ Because he did not want him to marry Lucie.

   B. ☐ Because he had not saved him from prison.

   C. ☐ Because he had denounced all the descendants of the Evrémonde family and Charles was a descendant.

   D. ☐ Because he did not know what he was writing when he was in prison.

9. Sydney Carton wants Lucie to leave Paris because
   A. ☐ he wants her to come to London where she can marry him after Charles is executed.
   B. ☐ he does not think she and her family will be safe in Paris now that Charles has been condemned.
   C. ☐ he thinks that he can help Charles more without her around.
   D. ☐ he does not want her to see him drinking.

10. Why does Madame Defarge wish to kill Lucie and Doctor Manette?
   A. ☐ Because she is not loyal to the Revolution.
   B. ☐ Because they are not loyal to the Revolution.
   C. ☐ Because she wants to destroy the Evrémonde family, and now Lucie and Doctor Manette are Evrémondes for her.
   D. ☐ Because Doctor Manette did not save her sister or her brother, and so now she wants to destroy his family.

What stops the wheel of revenge?

2 **The English poet W. H. Auden wrote a poem called 'September 1, 1939' in which he meditated [1] on the causes of the great world war that was about to begin. In the poem he wrote:**

I and the public know
What all schoolchildren learn,
Those to whom evil is done
Do evil in return.

a. How do these lines apply to the story of *A Tale of Two Cities*?
b. Dickens does show a way to stop this cycle of violence and revenge. What is it?

1. **meditated** : thought seriously.

'At extermination'[1]

3 When (in the original version of the novel) Monsieur Defarge asks his wife where their vengeance [2] should end, she responds, 'At extermination.' Obviously, with the violent and bloody history of the twentieth century in mind, these words still have a frightening and relevant ring to them. What is more, it is obvious that Charles Dickens portrays Madame Defarge as the 'villain', the evil person of the story. If you had written *A Tale of Two Cities*, would you have made her the villain?

In 200 words say why you would or would not have made a more sympathetic portrait of Madame Defarge.

Include the following information:

- the story of Madame Defarge's family
- how you would react if the same thing happened to your family
- how Dickens portrays Madame Defarge

You can begin like this:

In the novel 'A Tale of Two Cities' Charles Dickens presents Madame Defarge as...

---

1. **extermination** : complete destruction.
2. **vengeance** : revenge.

Before you go on

1 **Listen to the first part of Chapter Eleven, and fill in the gaps.**

Fifty-two prisoners were due to die the next ¹............................, and Charles Darnay was among them. He sat alone in his cell and ²............................ about what had happened. He was young and it was hard for him to accept that he had to ³............................ . He called the gaoler and bought paper and ink, intending to put his affairs in order before the next day.

He wrote a long ⁴............................ to Lucie, assuring her of his love. He explained that he had known ⁵............................ about her father's imprisonment, and nothing about what his father and ⁶............................ had done to the young peasant girl and her family. He ⁷............................ Lucie to comfort her father for the disaster that had overtaken them and to look after their ⁸............................ . Then he wrote to Doctor Manette. He told the doctor that he did not consider him in any way ⁹............................ for his death.

He ¹⁰............................ writing these letters and then lay down to sleep.

He ¹¹............................ early the next morning, and ¹²............................ to walk around the cell restlessly. He had never seen the ¹³............................ and he wondered what it looked ¹⁴............................ and exactly how he would be tied to it. The hours passed quickly. He heard nine o'clock strike and knew he would never hear it strike again. Then the clock ¹⁵............................ ten, and eleven, and twelve.

CHAPTER ELEVEN

Sydney Carton Plays his Last Card

Fifty-two prisoners were due to die the next day, and Charles Darnay was among them. He sat alone in his cell and thought about what had happened. He was young and it was hard for him to accept that he had to die. He called the gaoler and bought paper and ink, intending to put his affairs in order before the next day.

He wrote a long letter to Lucie, assuring her of his love. He explained that he had known nothing about her father's imprisonment, and nothing about what his father and uncle had done to the young peasant girl and her family. He told Lucie to comfort her father for the disaster that had overtaken [1] them and to look after their daughter. Then he wrote to Doctor Manette. He told the doctor that he did not consider him in any way responsible for his death.

He finished writing these letters and then lay down to sleep.

---

1. **overtaken** : struck.

A Tale of Two Cities

He woke early the next morning, and began to walk around the cell restlessly. [1] He had never seen the guillotine and he wondered what it looked like and exactly how he would be tied to it. The hours passed quickly. He heard nine o'clock strike and knew he would never hear it strike again. Then the clock struck ten, and eleven, and twelve. END

Just after one o'clock he heard footsteps outside in the corridor. The key was put in the lock and turned. Then he heard a voice whispering quickly in English.

'He's never seen me before. Go in alone – and be quick!'

The door opened and Sydney Carton came into the cell. He put his finger to his lips, to show that he wanted Darnay to remain silent. Then he stepped forward and shook the prisoner's hand eagerly. [2]

'Are you a prisoner, too?' Darnay asked him in dismay. [3]

'No. I have influence with one of the gaolers here, that's all. I've come from your wife. She has a request that she wants you to grant.' [4]

'What is it?'

'You must do what she asks,' Carton said urgently. 'There's no time to ask questions, no time for explanations. You must just do exactly what I tell you. Do you understand?'

Darnay nodded his head.

'Good. Now I want you to take off your boots and put on mine,' Carton ordered. 'And hurry – we haven't got much time.'

'Escape is impossible,' Darnay said. 'You'd only die with me if we tried it.'

'I'm not asking you to escape,' Carton replied. 'If I do ask you to

---

1. **restlessly** : moved constantly.
2. **eagerly** : (here) in a friendly way.
3. **in dismay** : with fear.
4. **grant** : agree to.

Sydney Carton Plays his last Card

escape, you can refuse. But now take this cravat [1] of mine and put it on. Give me yours.'

With great quickness Carton exchanged clothes with the prisoner. Darnay protested all the while, but the lawyer would not listen to him.

'It's madness to try it,' he kept saying. 'Don't throw away your life trying to save mine.'

'I'm not asking you to escape,' the lawyer repeated. 'If I do, you can always refuse.' He looked around the cell and saw the paper and ink on the table. 'Go to the table and write exactly what I tell you,' he commanded. 'Write exactly what I say – word for word.'

Darnay sat down at the table and picked up the pen.

'What shall I write?' the prisoner asked.

Carton began to dictate [2] the letter:

If you remember a conversation we had a long time ago, you will understand this when you see it.

As he dictated, Carton's hand moved into his jacket pocket and he took out a handkerchief. Suddenly he placed this handkerchief over Darnay's mouth and held it there tightly. The prisoner struggled [3] for a few seconds and then his head fell forward onto the table. He was asleep.

Carton went to the door of the cell and called softly. 'Come here.' John Barsad entered the cell. He was very nervous and frightened.

'You see?' Carton said, pointing to the unconscious Charles Darnay. 'Your danger is not so very great.'

'And will you keep your word?' [4] Barsad asked. 'Are you really

---

1. **cravat** :
2. **dictate** : speak something aloud for someone to write down.
3. **struggled** : (here) tried to free himself.
4. **word** : promise.

A Tale of Two Cities

determined to die for him, Mr Carton?'

'I'll keep my word,' the lawyer said firmly. 'No one will know that it's me who goes to the guillotine, and not Darnay. Now go and call for help,' he ordered. 'Tell the gaoler that Darnay's visitor was overcome with grief when he saw his old friend, and has fainted. Get the gaoler to help you carry him outside. Take him to Mr Lorry's house and put him in the carriage that's waiting there.'

A few minutes later Carton was alone in the cell. There was quietness around him and then he heard footsteps outside. Cell doors were thrown open, and harsh [1] commands could be heard. It was time!

The gaoler turned the key in the lock and gave the summons.

'Evrémonde, follow me!'

The prisoner left the cell and followed the gaoler into a large room. All the prisoners due to die that afternoon were gathered there. He stood in a dark corner by himself, worried that someone who knew the real Charles Darnay would see that he was an impostor. [2] He had been standing there for a few moments when a young girl came up to him. She peered at him in the darkness.

'It is me, Citizen Evrémonde,' she said. 'I am the seamstress [3] you met in the other prison.'

He bowed his head in greeting.

'May I ride with you, Citizen Evrémonde?' the girl asked humbly. 'It would give me courage to hold your hand.'

She raised her eyes to look into his face. Suddenly she gave a gasp and stepped back in confusion. Her eyes were wide open and she turned white. Carton put his finger to his lips.

'Are you dying for him?' she asked.

'And his wife and child,' the lawyer said.

---

1. **harsh** : rough.
2. **impostor** : person pretending to be somebody else.
3. **seamstress** : woman who sews for a living.

A Tale of Two Cities

The seamstress gazed [1] at him, lost in admiration.

'Let me stand by you and hold your hand!' she begged.

Carton put out his hand.

'To the end,' he promised firmly.

* * * *

While the prisoners waited for the tumbrils that would carry them to death, a carriage left Mr Lorry's house. The carriage drove to the gates of the city.

'Papers!' a voice cried.

The papers were handed over and the guard read them.

'Doctor Manette. Which one is he?'

Mr Lorry pointed to the old man.

'And his daughter Lucie. Where is she?'

Mr Lorry pointed again.

'Is this the child, Lucie?'

Mr Lorry nodded.

'Sydney Carton. Which one is he?'

Mr Lorry pointed at a figure lying in the corner of the carriage.

'Forward!'

1. **gazed** : looked for a long time.

Go back to the text

1 **Answer the following questions.**

    a. What did Charles wish to explain to Lucie before he died?

    b. What did he wish to explain to Doctor Manette?

    c. What did Charles think when he first saw Sydney Carton?

    d. Why isn't it a lie when Sydney says to Charles that he is 'not asking you to escape'?

    e. What does Sydney ask Charles to do?

    f. What conversation is Carton referring to?

    g. How does Charles 'escape'?

    h. Who recognises Sydney?

Verbs of perception

'He heard nine o'clock strike and knew he would never hear it strike again.'

Look at these sentences.

– *I heard the clock. It struck nine o'clock. = I heard the clock strike nine o'clock.*

– *I heard the tumbrils. They were rumbling along the street. = I heard the tumbrils rumbling along the street.*

– *He touched my arm. I felt it. = I felt him touch my arm.*

These verbs of perception *(to see, to hear, to feel)* can be followed by either the infinitive or ing-form of the verb.

As can be seen in the examples given above, in this construction:

– the ing-form corresponds to the Past Continuous. We use this form when we hear/see/feel someone in the middle of carrying out an action. We don't necessarily hear/see/feel the whole action.

– the infinitive corresponds to the Past Simple. We use this form for a complete action or for a short, immediate action.

2 **A.** **Combine the following sentences.**

Example: I heard him. He was screaming.
I heard him screaming.

a. The crowd yelled. He heard them.

b. The dog was barking under his window. He heard it.

c. I felt something in my hair. It was moving.

d. She felt the rain. It was splashing against her face.

e. The wind was whistling through the trees. He heard it.

f. The robber jumped out of the window. They saw him.

g. The judge called for silence in the courtroom. The lawyer heard him.

h. The children were running up and down the stairs. We saw them.

B. Fill in the gaps with either the infinitive or ing-form of the verbs given according to the context.

Example: I saw him (*die*) ....die........ on the guillotine.

a. There was not much light in the room but I could see her (*write*) .... a letter.

b. I was at the Bastille on July 14, and I saw him (*fall down*) .... dead. A soldier had shot him through the heart.

c. I went to the concert last night and I heard her (*sing*) .... that song.

d. She was in bed reading *A Tale of Two Cities* when she heard a bottle (*break*) .... She got out of bed and went downstairs, and saw her children (*watch*) .... a film on TV. Her youngest child turned around and saw their mother (*look*) .... at them.

e. The soldier felt a warm liquid (*flow*) .... down his arm. For a second he thought it was blood.

f. I walked into the house and saw a candle (*burn*) .... in the drawing-room. I walked into the drawing-room and all of a sudden I heard someone (*shout*) ...., 'Who goes there? Friend or foe?' [1]

g. Last year a friend of mine and I went into that church to look at its paintings. As we were admiring the paintings we heard a chamber orchestra (*play*) .... some music by Bach. 'How strange,' said my friend, 'recorded music in a church!' Just then we turned a corner and saw a real chamber orchestra in the church (*practise*) .... for their concert that night.

h. Charles was walking into the shop when he felt somebody (*bump*) .... into him.

---

1. **foe** : enemy.

CHAPTER TWELVE

A Flash and a Crash

Madame Defarge was talking to her woman friend Vengeance and to Jacques Three.

'Defarge is a good republican and a brave man,' Madame Defarge said, 'but he has certain weaknesses. He feels sorry for Doctor Manette.'

'That's a shame,' Jacques Three said solemnly. 'A good citizen should not feel sorry.'

Madame Defarge raised her hand for silence. Jacques Three was instantly quiet.

'I don't mind about the doctor,' Madame Defarge said. 'He can go free for all that I care – but Evrémonde's family is a different matter. The wife and child must die!'

'The wife is beautiful,' Jacques Three commented. 'She would look good on the guillotine.' He rubbed his hands together eagerly. 'It'd be a pretty sight.'

'I'm afraid my husband may warn them,' Madame Defarge said

A Flash and a Crash

ominously. [1] 'I'm going to visit the wife now. She will be sad at Evrémonde's death and may say something against the Republic. That will give us the chance we need!'

'What a woman you are!' Vengeance cried in admiration.

'Indeed!' Jacques Three agreed with her. 'And a real friend to the Republic.'

2

'Take my knitting,' Madame Defarge told Vengeance. 'Keep my usual seat for me. I'll join you before the executions begin.'

'You won't be late?' Vengeance asked anxiously. 'You'll be there before the tumbrils arrive, won't you? Before they arrive,' she repeated excitedly.

Madame Defarge nodded and then she walked away from her two friends. She carried a pistol and a knife hidden in her clothes

3

and her heart was fixed on [2] hatred and revenge.

---

1. **ominously** : with a feeling that something bad is going to happen.
2. **fixed on** : determined on.

A Tale of Two Cities

Mr Lorry had made his plans carefully the night before. He had decided that Miss Pross and Jerry should leave Paris at three o'clock in a small carriage. They would join the coach with the other passengers as soon as they could on the road outside Paris.

As Madame Defarge was making her way through the streets to the house, Jerry and Miss Pross were making plans of their own. They had seen Charles Darnay being put into the coach and they had seen the coach drive away.

'I'm so worried about them,' Miss Pross said tearfully. 'They must get away safely, Mr Cruncher! But if the people see a second carriage leaving the house, they may get suspicious. That's what worries me, Mr Cruncher. I think you should go out and stop the vehicle and horses from coming here. Take them to the cathedral,' she suggested. 'Wait for me there. That would be best, wouldn't it, Mr Cruncher?'

'Perhaps you're right, ma'am,' Jerry agreed. 'But I'd rather not leave you here alone,' he added doubtfully.

'Don't worry about me,' Miss Pross told him quickly. 'Wait for me at the cathedral at three o'clock, Mr Cruncher.'

Jerry left the house at twenty past two, and Miss Pross went inside to get ready for the journey. She was very nervous and kept looking around to make sure that no one had come into the house. As she walked from one room to another, she became aware that there was someone else in the house. She looked around in panic – and saw Madame Defarge standing next to her!

Madame Defarge looked coldly at the Englishwoman.

'Where is Evrémonde's wife?' she demanded.

Miss Pross thought quickly. All the doors were open. If Madame Defarge looked into the rooms, she would immediately see that the family had gone. There were four doors in the room. Miss Pross closed them all. Then she stood with her back to the

A Flash and a Crash

door that had been Lucie's bedroom. Madame Defarge watched Miss Pross suspiciously. The two women stared at each other with instinctive distrust.

'You might be the wife of Lucifer,' Miss Pross commented, 'but I am an Englishwoman. You won't get past me.'

Madame Defarge knew that Miss Pross was devoted [1] to the family. For her part, Miss Pross knew that Madame Defarge was the family's enemy.

'I'm on my way to the executions,' Madame Defarge said. 'I have come to say hello to Evrémonde's wife. Where is she?'

'I know you're an evil woman,' Miss Pross replied, 'but I'll fight you to the end.'

Each woman spoke her own language and neither of them understood a word of what the other said. They looked at each other with defiance [2] and hatred and they did not need words to understand that a terrible battle was going on between them.

'Evrémonde's wife should not hide herself away from me,' Madame Defarge said. 'It could be dangerous for her to hide – people might think she was an enemy of the Republic. Where is she?'

'I'll never give in to you,' Miss Pross replied. 'I'll fight you to the end, you wicked woman.'

Madame Defarge understood from the tone of Miss Pross' voice that she was in the presence of an enemy.

'Fool!' she cried out in anger. 'You don't matter to me. [3] It's Evrémonde's wife I want. Take me to her immediately, or get out of my way!'

Madame Defarge took a step forward towards the door of Lucie's room. Miss Pross braced herself [4] for the struggle. The two women

---

1. **devoted** : loyal.
2. **defiance** : aggression.
3. **You don't matter to me** : You're not important to me.
4. **braced herself** : prepared herself.

A Tale of Two Cities

continued to stare at each other.

'Doctor Manette! Evrémonde's wife! Where are you?'

There was no reply to Madame Defarge's sudden call. She continued to look at Miss Pross and then Madame Defarge understood that they had gone. She ran quickly around the room and opened three of the four doors. She could see that possessions had been removed from the rooms. She turned angrily to Miss Pross.

'There is no one in that room behind you,' she said accusingly. 'Let me look.'

'Never,' Miss Pross announced firmly. She understood exactly what Madame Defarge wanted.

'If they're not there in that room, I can have them brought back to Paris,' Madame Defarge said to herself.

'As long as you don't know whether they're in that room or not, you don't know what to do,' Miss Pross said to herself. 'And I'll never let you leave this house.'

'Get away from the door,' Madame Defarge said threateningly.

She moved suddenly towards Miss Pross. Miss Pross took hold of the Frenchwoman around the waist and held on to her tightly. Madame Defarge struggled wildly, and scratched Miss Pross' face cruelly with her nails. Miss Pross continued holding her.

Madame Defarge felt inside her clothing for her pistol. She drew [1] the weapon out, and prepared to fire at Miss Pross. The Englishwoman saw the pistol and knocked it out of her enemy's hand. Miss Pross saw a flash of light and she heard a crash – then she found herself standing alone in the room. Madame Defarge was lying at her feet. She looked down. Madame Defarge was dead.

Miss Pross looked at the body of her enemy for a few minutes and then she turned her mind to what she needed to do next. She

---

1. **drew** : took.

A Flash and a Crash

put on a bonnet [1] and veil that covered the terrible scratches on her face and walked out of the house. She walked quickly to the cathedral and waited for Jerry to come with the carriage. She had not been waiting for more than five minutes when he arrived. She climbed into the carriage hurriedly and they drove away.

'Is there any noise in the streets?' Miss Pross asked anxiously.

'Just the usual noises,' Jerry told her.

'I can't hear you,' Miss Pross said. 'What did you say?'

Jerry looked at her in surprise. He noticed the marks on her face and he saw her clothing was torn and disordered. [2]

'Is there any noise in the streets now?' she asked again.

Jerry nodded at her. He could hear the tumbrils rolling heavily through the streets, carrying the prisoners to the guillotine.

'There's the roll of those dreadful carts,' he told her. 'Can you hear that, miss?'

'I can't hear anything,' she said softly. 'There was a flash and a crash. After that there was a great stillness, and I don't think I'll ever hear anything again as long as I live.'

'If she can't hear the roll of those dreadful carts, she never will hear anything else in this world,' Jerry thought.

And indeed she never did.

1.   **bonnet :**
2.   **disordered** : untidy.

131

Go back to the text

FCE **1** Chapter Twelve has been divided into eight parts. Choose the most suitable heading from the list A-I for each part (1-8). There is one extra heading which you do not need to use.

- **A** ☐ All understood understanding nothing
- **B** ☐ Dead quiet
- **C** ☐ The servants decide on their own
- **D** ☐ A place at the show
- **E** ☐ All's right in the world
- **F** ☐ England 1, France 0
- **G** ☐ They might be there, or they might not
- **H** ☐ Humane sentiments are out
- **I** ☐ A surprise visit

A genius[1] of description

2 Charles Dickens was certainly not an intellectual and analytical writer, and for this reason many intellectual professors have criticised his writings. Still, as many famous writers of the past and present have noted, Dickens had a genius for description. No writer can make people, objects and scenes come alive like he could.

This chapter contains two examples of this genius.

A. How does Dickens make the deadly meeting between Madame Defarge and Miss Pross even more memorable?

B. How does Dickens communicate to us the monumental nature of Miss Pross's sacrifice?

---

1. **genius** : a person who has great mental skill or artistic ability.

I'd rather

I'd rather not leave you here alone.

Look at these sentences:

I'd rather not leave you here alone. = *I'd prefer not to leave... .*
I'd rather have chicken for dinner. = *I would prefer to have chicken for dinner.*

But if you are talking about what you want somebody else to do:
Subject + *would rather* + subject + Past Simple.

| I | *would rather* | *you* | *knew* | *who I really am.* |

Remember:

'I'd rather' is the short form of 'I would rather'.

3 **A. Rewrite the sentences with *I'd prefer to* with *I'd rather*, and the sentences with *I'd rather* with *I'd prefer to*. Notice that *rather* in this construction is not followed by *to*.**

    a. I'd rather eat at home tonight.

    ....

    b. I'd prefer to go to the cinema.

    ....

    c. I'd prefer to read a mystery story.

    ....

    d. I'd rather talk about it another time.

    ....

    e. I'd prefer not to do it.

    ....

    f. I'd rather go home.

    ....

B. **Complete the following sentences with the name of the character and the right verb according to the context. The sentence should make sense according to what you know about the character.**

Madame Defarge   Mr Cruncher
Charles Darnay   Doctor Manette
Sydney Carton   Mr Lorry
Monseigneur   Monsieur Defarge
Miss Pross   Marquis St Evrémonde

> show   torture   taste   knit   do   examine
>   keep   teach   defend   take

Example:

I can *taste* this hot chocolate but *I'd rather Monseigneur tasted it.*

a. We can .... you at the treason trial, but we
....

b. I can .... your message to Dover, but
....

c. I can .... you a pullover, but
....

d. I can .... you French grammar, but
....

e. I can .... the shopping, but
....

f. We can .... the peasants, but
....

g. I can .... valuables in a safe place, but
....

h. I can .... the letter Doctor Manette wrote in
prison, but ....

i. I can .... that sick woman, but
....

How Dickens interpreted[1] the French Revolution

A *Tale of Two Cities* is not a political novel in the conventional sense. Dickens was not interested in the political debates of the period, or the ideas of the revolutionaries. He mentioned nothing about the National Assembly or the attempt to establish a constitutional monarchy. He made very few references to the democratic ideas centred on the rights of man. He focused instead on how the Revolution affected the lives of individuals who were caught up in it.

This does not mean that Dickens avoided all political comment. He attacked aristocratic privilege and abuse,[2] which he saw as the main causes of the Revolution. The aristocratic class was generally portrayed as irresponsible, self-indulgent[3] and corrupt. They were interested in their own welfare rather than the well-being of France. They made no contribution to the economic life of the country because they did not pay taxes. The earlier generation of the Evrémonde family were cruel individuals who took the maximum advantage of their wealth and status. They treated the peasants

---

1. **interpreted** : explained the meaning of something.
2. **abuse** : cruel or violent treatment.
3. **self - indulgent** : allowing yourself to do what you enjoy, instead of controlling your desires.

badly, keeping them in poverty and fear, and they abused the power they had for personal pleasure or to punish their enemies. The story of Doctor Manette's imprisonment, and the reasons for it, illustrate Dickens's attitude towards the French aristocracy.

The attack on the Bastille is described in *A Tale of Two Cities*, and it represents a pivotal [1] point in the novel. Up to that point Dickens had been sympathetic [2] to the sufferings of the people and harsh in

---

1. **pivotal** : central, vital. 2. **sympathetic** : showing pity.

Last Victims of Terror (1794) by Ch. L. Muller. Aristocrats and royalists await their turn at the guillotine.

Mary Evans Picture Library.

his criticisms of the privileged. With the attack on the Bastille, however, his attitude changed.

This change of attitude can be most clearly seen in the portrayal of Madame Defarge. She was very much a background figure until the storming of the Bastille. There, however, she led the women of Paris in the attack. From then on, she became a devotee [1] of the guillotine and showed no pity for those who were going to be executed.

Although Dickens recognised that the conditions of life in pre-Revolutionary France were terrible for ordinary people, his attitude hardened as the Revolution became increasingly violent. By the end of the novel, it is clear that his sympathies for the Revolutionaries had turned to horror at their violence.

1 **Answer the following questions.**

    a. What aspects of the French Revolution are not discussed in *A Tale of Two Cities*?

    b. What aspect of the French Revolution is discussed in *A Tale of Two Cities*?

    c. How does Dickens present the French aristocracy?

    d. Which part of the novel illustrates Dickens's attitude towards the aristocracy?

    e. At what point in the novel does Dickens's attitude towards the French people change?

    f. What changed Dickens's feelings towards the French Revolution?

---

1.   **devotee** : fan, supporter.

Before you go on

1 **Read the text below. Use the word given in capitals at the end of the lines to form a word that fits in the gap: turn a noun into an adjective, an adjective into an adverb, a comparative adjective into a superlative, etc. There is an example at the beginning (0).**

The tumbrils rolled **0**.......noisily........ through the Paris streets. There were six of them that day, each containing the **1**......................... prisoners who were going to die for the Republic.

Some of the **2**......................... looked out at the city with interest as they were carried through the streets. Others were too **3**......................... to look up. One man had been driven mad by his **4**......................... and he began to sing and dance.

The crowd pushed close against the tumbrils and many people asked the guard which prisoner was the **5**......................... Evrémonde. The guard pointed to a man who was standing up at the back of one of the vehicles. The man was listening to a young girl who was telling him something with great **6**......................... .

The spy was waiting when the tumbrils reached the end of their journey to the guillotine. He looked **7**......................... to see that the prisoner was still there. He had been afraid that the bargain would be broken. A man standing next to him asked which prisoner was Evrémonde.

'There. At the back,' the spy replied.

'Down with Evrémonde!' the man cried **8**................ .

'Hush, hush!' the spy said in a **9**......................... voice.

The man looked at him in surprise.

'He'll be dead in five minutes,' Barsad explained

NOISE	
HAPPY	
PRISON	
MISERY	
SUFFER	
FAME	
INTENSE	
ANXIOUS	
LOUD	
FRIGHT	

10........................ . 'Let him die in peace.'   QUIET

The man sneered 11........................ and went on   CONTEMPT
shouting.

'Death to Evrémonde! Death to Evrémonde!'

The prisoner looked for a moment into the face of
the man who was shouting and then he
12........................ the spy. He stared closely at the   RECOGNITION
spy's face.

The tumbrils drew up to the guillotine. The place
of 13........................ contained a number of chairs   EXECUTE
and the people of Paris were sitting there waiting
for the prisoners.

 Now listen to the recording and check your answers.

CHAPTER THIRTEEN

The Guillotine

The tumbrils rolled noisily through the Paris streets. There were six of them that day, each containing the unhappy prisoners who were going to die for the Republic.

Some of the prisoners looked out at the city with interest as they were carried through the streets. Others were too miserable to look up. One man had been driven mad by his sufferings and he began to sing and dance.

The crowd pushed close against the tumbrils and many people asked the guard which prisoner was the famous Evrémonde. The guard pointed to a man who was standing up at the back of one of the vehicles. The man was listening to a young girl who was telling him something with great intensity.

The spy was waiting when the tumbrils reached the end of their journey to the guillotine. He looked anxiously to see that the prisoner was still there. He had been afraid that the bargain would be broken. A man standing next to him asked which prisoner was Evrémonde.

'There. At the back,' the spy replied.

The Guillotine

'Down with Evrémonde!' the man cried loudly.

'Hush, hush!' the spy said in a frightened voice.

The man looked at him in surprise.

'He'll be dead in five minutes,' Barsad explained quietly. 'Let him die in peace.'

The man sneered contemptuously and went on shouting.

'Death to Evrémonde! Death to Evrémonde!'

The prisoner looked for a moment into the face of the man who was shouting and then he recognised the spy. He stared closely at the spy's face.

The tumbrils drew up to the guillotine. The place of execution contained a number of chairs and the people of Paris were sitting there waiting for the prisoners. Madame Defarge's friend, Vengeance, was sitting in the front row and she had put her friend's knitting on an empty chair by her side.

A Tale of Two Cities

'Where is she?' Vengeance wondered. 'If she doesn't come soon, she'll miss it all.'

The first prisoner was led to the guillotine. He lay down on the awful machine. There was a crash! The executioner held up a bloody head for the crowd to see. The women stopped their knitting for a moment and counted: 'One.'

At last it was the turn of those in the third tumbril. The prisoner called Evrémonde stepped down to the ground and turned to help the seamstress down. He made her stand with her back to the guillotine. She looked into his face.

'You have helped me to be strong,' she told him.

'Keep your eyes on me,' Sydney Carton replied. 'Don't look at anything else.'

'Is it time?' she asked. 'Is it time now?'

'Yes.'

She kissed him and moved away towards the guillotine. In a moment her life was over.

Sydney Carton spent his last few moments thinking of the people he was leaving behind.

'They will be happy,' he told himself. 'She will have another child and she will give that child my name. The child will grow into a fine man and will follow the same path that I did. I see him making my name famous as he achieves success. His successes will wipe away the stains [1] of my name. I can see him when he is older, bringing his own son here to Paris. I see them looking at this spot and the father telling his child my story with a tender voice.'

---

1. **stains** : dishonourable memories.

Go back to the text

1 **Say whether the following statements are True (T) or False (F), and then correct the false ones.**

		T	F

a. One prisoner going to the guillotine sang and danced because he was happy to die. ☐ ☐

b. Barsad told the man shouting 'Down with Evrémonde' to be quiet because he wanted Sydney to be able to die in peace. ☐ ☐

c. Vengeance did not know that her friend, Madame Defarge, was dead. ☐ ☐

d. Sydney Carton gave the seamstress the courage to die on the guillotine. ☐ ☐

e. Sydney Carton is worried that Lucie and her son will lead sad lives. ☐ ☐

f. Sydney Carton imagines Lucie's grandson coming to the place where Sydney will meet his death. ☐ ☐

Summing it all up

2 **Number the paragraphs in the right order to make a summary of Chapters 9-13, and then fill in the gaps with the words given below.**

cravat   studying   brother   wipe   son-in-law   Barsad
descendants   drew   kiss   taken   tumbril   cell   traitor
spy   accuser   dismay   Charles   death   scratched
Paris   Pross   escape   beaten   crash   account   boots

a. ☐ At first John Barsad said he would not help, but Sydney Carton told him that he would reveal that he had been a ¹..................... for the British government. If the French knew this they would consider him a ²..................... . John Barsad realised that he was ³..................... and so he said he would help. However, Barsad refused to do anything too dangerous and he told Sydney Carton that ⁴..................... was impossible.

b. ☐ Jerry, too, had been 5..................... Miss Pross's brother and said that he recognised him. But he could only remember his first name, John. Just then they all heard someone utter the surname, 6..................... . It was Sydney Carton, and he explained that he was searching for a friend in the gaol to help Charles Darnay and this friend was Solomon 7..................... .

c. ☐ After this, the second trial against Charles Darnay began. This time, though, the situation was even worse, and when it was revealed that his third 8..................... was Doctor Manette it was clear that Charles would be condemned to the guillotine. Of course, Doctor Manette did not willingly accuse his 9....................., but he had written a long letter when he was a prisoner. This letter was found by Monsieur Defarge in Doctor Manette's 10..................... when the Bastille was 11..................... . This letter contained a full 12..................... of why he was in prison and all the horrible things the Evrémonde family had done. Doctor Manette ended his letter by denouncing the Evrémondes and all their 13..................... .

d. ☐ Then it was his turn, but he died with the thought that he was helping Lucie's future. He thought that she would have another child and that she would name this son after him. This son would grow up to be a success and so 14..................... out the stain of Sydney Carton's name. Then Lucie's son would have a son, and he would take him to 15..................... where he would tell him the story of Sydney Carton's last days. So, with these thoughts, Sydney Carton consoled [1] himself before he died.

e. ☐ Charles Darnay looked at him in 16.....................: he thought that he too was a prisoner. Sydney Carton said that he had come to carry out Lucie's wishes. Then, Sydney Carton put a handkerchief over Charles' mouth, which had some substance that made him fall asleep. He then had Charles carried out of the prison and onto a carriage with Doctor Manette, Lucie and their child.

f. ☐ After Charles Darnay was arrested the second time, Jerry Cruncher and Miss Pross entered a wine shop where Miss Pross was shocked to see her 17..................... . She cried his name, Solomon, but he did not seem very happy to see her. He explained that he was an official of the Revolutionary government, and if they were seen together it would be the 18..................... of him.

g. ☐ After Charles was found guilty for the second time and condemned to

---

1. **consoled** : comforted.

the guillotine, Sydney Carton went to Mr Lorry to tell him of his plan to get Lucie, her daughter and Doctor Manette out of Paris safely. On the day of the execution Sydney Carton went to visit [19].................... in his cell.

h. ☐ Meanwhile, Lucie, her daughter, Doctor Manette and Charles Darnay escaped from Paris, and that same afternoon Sydney Carton, whom the crowd thought was Charles, was taken from the prison to the guillotine to be executed. He had ridden on the [20].................... with a young seamstress. When it was her turn to die he told her to look at him and not at the guillotine. She gave him a [21].................... and then went to die.

i. ☐ Everything was going according to Sydney Carton's plan, but Madame Defarge decided to try to have Lucie arrested as an enemy of the Republic. Fortunately Miss Pross arrived at Lucie's house before Madame Defarge. Miss Pross stood in front of Lucie's room and made it clear that she would not let Madame Defarge enter. Finally the two women began to fight. While they were fighting, Madame Defarge [22].................... out her pistol, but Miss Pross knocked it out of her hand and there was a flash and a [23].................... . Madame Defarge was killed by her own pistol and Miss Pross became deaf forever.

A modern Dickens

3 **Read about the mystery writer and then discover his name by doing the puzzle.**

Our mystery writer is a great fan of Charles Dickens. He says that Dickens' novel *Great Expectations* was the first novel he read that he wished he had written. He particularly enjoys Dickens' complex and 'unlikely' plots and bizarre characters. Indeed, this writer's novels are famous for their grotesque [1] characters and incredible plots, and he most definitely does not agree with America's great novelist Ernest Hemingway who said that writers should only write about what they know personally. He thinks that we modern readers are too emotionally restrained.

He was born in Exeter, New Hampshire in 1942, and later attended the University of Pittsburgh and the University of New Hampshire. He also

1. **grotesque** : strange and unpleasant.

went to Vienna for a study-abroad program where he had the good luck to study with the German novelist Gunter Grass. His first teaching job was at Mount Holyoke College in 1967 and his first novel, *Setting Free the Bears*, was published in 1969.

He gained real fame when his 1978 novel *The World According to Garp* was made into a successful film starring Robin Williams and Glenn Close. Since then other novels of his have been made into films, including *The Hotel New Hampshire* and *The Cider House Rules*.

Although like Dickens he is keenly interested in social and political issues, his novels concentrate on other things. 'It is never,' he said, 'the social or political relationship that interests me in a novel. I begin with an interest in a relationship, a situation, a character.'

So, if you are not embarrassed by the great tear-jerking [1] scene of Sydney Carton before the guillotine, sacrificing himself for a woman who could never love him, then perhaps this mystery writer will be to your liking too.

1. The crowd was shouting at him with anger and disgust. The crowd was...

2. A woman's hat (also in the United Kingdom it is the lid covering the motor of a car, which in the United States is called the 'hood').

3. What a pity! = What a ...! (this word also means a kind of embarrassment for something).

4. Defeated.

5. The famous carts, once used for harmless things like carrying barrels of wine, but which were used to carry men and women to the guillotines.

6. Say something or make a sound like a word.

7. A kind of neck tie.

8. A feeling of hopelessness and discouragement.

9. A report.

10. Shocking.

1 ☐☐☐☐☐☐☐
2 ☐☐☐☐☐
3 ☐☐☐☐
4 ☐☐☐☐☐☐
5 ☐☐☐☐☐☐☐
6 ☐☐☐☐☐
7 ☐☐☐☐☐
8 ☐☐☐☐☐☐
9 ☐☐☐☐☐☐
10 ☐☐☐☐☐☐☐☐

1.   **tear-jerking** : making people cry.

EXIT TEST

Choose the right answers, (A, B, C or D) for the following questions.

1. What did Mr Lorry mean by his message, 'Recalled to life'?
   A. ☐ That Doctor Manette had been released from prison.
   B. ☐ That Lucie Manette would now become part of Doctor Manette's life again.
   C. ☐ That he had discovered that Doctor Manette was not really dead, but had been in prison.
   D. ☐ That Lucie Manette was finally going back to her life in Paris.

2. How did Mr Lorry first meet Doctor Manette?
   A. ☐ He managed the financial affairs of Doctor Manette and his wife.
   B. ☐ He was a good friend of Lucie's.
   C. ☐ He was introduced to him by Monsieur Defarge.
   D. ☐ They were both travelling on the same boat from Dover to France.

3. Why was Doctor Manette in Monsieur Defarge's care when he first got out of prison?
   A. ☐ Because Monsieur Defarge saw him as a hero of the French Revolution.
   B. ☐ Because he had been Doctor Manette's servant.
   C. ☐ Because Monsieur Defarge worked for the Paris branch of Tellson's bank.
   D. ☐ Because he needed the shoes that Doctor Manette made.

4. Why was Charles Darnay on trial in England?
   A. ☐ For spying.
   B. ☐ For debt.
   C. ☐ For gambling.
   D. ☐ For lying to an English court.

5. What coincidence helped to get Charles Darnay acquitted in the English trial?

   A. ☐ The fact that he and Mr Lorry were on the same mail travelling to Dover.

   B. ☐ The fact that he and Mr Lorry were on the same boat travelling to England.

   C. ☐ The fact that he and Sydney Carton resembled each other.

   D. ☐ The fact that he and John Barsad resembled each other.

6. What was the Marquis's main worry when his carriage ran over Jacques's child?

   A. ☐ That he was responsible for the death of an innocent child.

   B. ☐ That his nephew, Charles Darnay, would be angry with him.

   C. ☐ That Jacques would try to kill him.

   D. ☐ That his horses were hurt.

7. Why was Doctor Manette pale and trembling after Charles Darnay told him his real name?

   A. ☐ Because he realised that Charles Darnay was a member of the French aristocracy.

   B. ☐ Because he realised that he was the son of one of the men who was responsible for putting him in prison.

   C. ☐ Because he realised that Charles Darnay was a liar.

   D. ☐ Because he realised that Charles Darnay would one day take his daughter back to France.

8. Why did Charles Darnay decide to go to France after the Revolution had begun?

   A. ☐ Because he wanted to fight for the aristocracy.

   B. ☐ Because he wanted to fight for the Revolution.

   C. ☐ Because he was afraid the English would think he was a spy.

   D. ☐ Because he felt that he had to help a servant of his family who was in prison.

9. Why was Doctor Manette considered a hero of the French Revolution?

   A. ☐ Because he had been a prisoner of the Bastille for many years.

   B. ☐ Because he had helped to conquer the Bastille.

C. ☐ Because Monsieur Defarge had been his servant.

D. ☐ Because he saved the lives of many people when he had worked as a doctor.

10. How did Charles Darnay's English trial help him to get acquitted during his French trial?

A. ☐ He was tried in England as a spy: this showed that he was not a friend of the English aristocratic regime.

B. ☐ He was tried in England as a spy: this showed that he had a job, unlike the real French aristocrats.

C. ☐ The English acquitted him: this showed that he was not really a bad person.

D. ☐ Doctor Manette had testified in his favour during the English trial: this showed that Charles must be a friend of the French Revolution.

11. Why did Doctor Manette accuse Charles Darnay?

A. ☐ Because he had discovered that Charles' father and uncle had been responsible for placing him in the Bastille.

B. ☐ Because he did not approve of his marriage with Lucie.

C. ☐ Because he had denounced all the descendants of the Evrémonde family.

D. ☐ Because he thought that Charles was a bad person since he resembled Sydney Carton.

12. How did Sydney Carton convince Solomon Pross to help him?

A. ☐ Sydney Carton told Solomon that he would tell the French that he was English.

B. ☐ Sydney Carton told Solomon that he would tell the French that he had been in debtors' prison.

C. ☐ Sydney Carton told Solomon that he would tell the French that he had been an informer for the English.

D. ☐ Sydney Carton told Solomon that he would tell the French that his sister worked for Mr Lorry.

13. Why was Doctor Manette placed in prison?

A. ☐ Because he had tried to help the poor people that the Evrémonde brothers had hurt.

B. ☐ Because he had been a friend of the Evrémonde brothers.

C. ☐ Because he had tried to tell the authorities what the Evrémonde brothers had done.

D. ☐ Because Charles's mother was afraid that he would tell the authorities what her husband had done.

14. Whom did Sydney think would one day tell his story?

A. ☐ Lucie

B. ☐ Lucie's daughter

C. ☐ Lucie's son

D. ☐ Doctor Manette

2 Shades of Meaning
In *A Tale of Two Cities* an accurate interpretation of certain phrases and sentences is essential to the story.

a. Why does Mr Lorry keep saying that it was 'just a business relationship' when he talks about Lucie's family?

b. Why is Sydney Carton telling the truth when he tells Solomon that he doesn't want Darnay to 'escape' from the prison?

c. What is the irony of the note left by the murderer of Marquis Evrémonde: 'Drive him fast to his tomb, Jacques'?

3 A Tale of Two Treasons
Charles Darnay is accused of treason by both the English and the French. What do these two trials have in common with regard to:

a. the way the authorities try to condemn him?

b. the punishment that he will receive?

4 Things in Common

a. What do Madame Defarge and Doctor Manette have in common?

b. What do Sydney Carton and Charles Darnay have in common?

5 Sacrifice

a. What is Doctor Manette's great sacrifice for his daughter?

b. What does Charles Darnay sacrifice?

c. What does Miss Pross sacrifice?

6 Symbols
What do the following things symbolise?

a. the wine barrel that falls in the street

b. the making of hot chocolate

c. Miss Pross's inability to hear the tumbrils

FCE EXIT TEST

PAPER 1

Reading Comprehension

Part 1

You are going to read an adaptation of part of Charles Dickens's short story 'The Schoolboy's Story' about a student at a boarding school. Choose the most suitable heading from the list A-H for each part (1-6). There is one extra heading which you do not need to use. There is an example at the beginning (0).

A. Tears of happiness and tears of sadness

B. Boys and food are not the same

C. A smile that makes you angry

D. Bad meals mean bad health

E. A bad beginning

F. Visiting a sad friend

G. Summer fun

H. The phantom with a stomach-ache

THE SCHOOLBOY'S STORY

I want to tell you about Old Cheeseman. He is one of the students at our school, and believe me the food which they serve us is terrible. The beef is impossible to chew and the beer makes us sick. One of the students had to go back home because he was ill. The doctor said it was the beef and I can believe it.

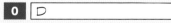
0 ⟦D⟧

However, beef and Old Cheeseman are two different things. It was Old Cheeseman that I wanted to talk about and not how our health is ruined because the school wants to make profit.

1 ⟦   ⟧

Old Cheeseman one night walked in his sleep, put his hat on and got a fishing rod and went down into the main living-room, where they naturally thought that he was a ghost. But he never would have done that if his meals had been healthy. When we all begin to walk in our sleep, I suppose they will be sorry for it.

2 ⟦   ⟧

Old Cheeseman first came to the school when he was very small in a carriage with a woman who was always shaking him. This is all I remember about it. He never went home for the holidays. He had two suits of clothing each year, and his shoes were always too big for him.

3 [_____]

During the summer holidays some of the students who lived near the school came to say hello to Old Cheeseman. When they said to him, 'Halloa, Old Cheeseman, what have you had for dinner?' he said, 'Boiled beef.' And when they said, 'Aren't you lonely here all by yourself?' He said, 'Yes, it is a bit boring sometimes.'

4 [_____]

But that was not the end of his troubles. When the other students came back from the holidays, not wanting to at all, he was happy to see them. Now this always made them angry because they were not all happy to see him, and so he got his head knocked against walls, and that was the way his nose bled.

5 [_____]

Still, he was a favourite in general, and once we collected money for him, and bought him two white mice, a rabbit, a pigeon and a beautiful puppy so that he would not be so lonely during the holidays. Old Cheeseman was so happy about our gift that he cried – especially a little bit later when these animals all ate one another.

6 [_____]

Part 2

You are going to read Charles Dickens's true account of an Italian political prisoner, adapted from a text from *The Uncommercial Traveller*. For questions 7-14 choose the correct answers, (A, B, C or D).

THE ITALIAN PRISONER

Before I went to Italy a friend of mine, who is a very good and kind man, told me to visit Giovanni Carlavero when I was there. My friend had saved Giovanni Carlavero's life some years ago.

Giovanni Carlavero had fought for Italy's independence and so he was a political prisoner in the North of Italy. He was condemned for life, and he certainly would have died in prison if my English friend had not seen him.

It happened that my English friend visited that horrible and old prison; part of it was below the waterline of the harbour. The room where Giovanni was imprisoned received hardly any air or light. The condition was incredibly horrendous and my friend could barely breathe inside and could see only with the help of a torch. At the upper end of the prison room, and so in the worst position, since it was the farthest away from light and air, the Englishman first saw him. He was on an iron bed, to which he was chained by a heavy chain.

The Englishman did not think that he looked anything like any of the other criminals in the room, and so he talked with him, and learnt how he came to be there.

When the Englishman emerged from the dreadful cell, he asked the governor of the jail why Giovanni Carlavero was put in the worst part of the prison.

'Because he is particularly recommended,' was the short answer.

'Recommended, that is to say, for death?' asked my friend.

'Excuse me, particularly recommended,' was again the answer.

'He has a bad tumour in his neck,' continued my friend, 'and if he continues to stay in that dark, wet cell, it will kill him.'

'Excuse me, I can do nothing. He is particularly recommended.'

The Englishman was living in that town, and he went to his home there, but the figure of this man chained to the iron bed made it no home, and destroyed his rest and peace. He was an Englishman of an extraordinarily tender heart, and he could not bear the picture. So he began to visit that man often, and he even treated his tumour.

One day, when all the town knew about the Englishman and his political prisoner, an Italian barrister came to my friend with a strange proposal.

'Give me a hundred pounds to obtain Carlavero's freedom. I think I can get him a pardon with that money. But I cannot tell you what I am going to do with the money, and you must never ask me any questions.'

The Englishman decided to risk the hundred pounds. He did so, and did not hear another word of the matter. For half a year and more, the barrister never communicated with the Englishman in any way. Then the Englishman had to move to another town in the North of Italy. He was very sad to leave the prisoner.

The Englishman lived in this new town for another half-year and had no news of the prisoner. Finally, he received a calm, short, mysterious note saying, 'If you still want to free your friend the political prisoner, send me fifty pounds more, and I think I can do it.'

This time, though, the Englishman did not send the money. He wrote the barrister a letter saying that he knew that he had been tricked. Then he decided to walk to the post-office and post the letter. It was a lovely spring day. The sky was exquisitely blue and the sea divinely beautiful. As he walked to the post-office he was moved by the beauty of the scene and by the thought of the slowly dying prisoner who would never again enjoy such a wonderful day. So, he threw away that letter and sent the barrister another letter with the fifty pounds.

Within a week, the Englishman was having his breakfast when he heard some sounds on the staircase, and then Giovanni Carlavero jumped into the room and embraced the Englishman, a free man!

Conscious of having wronged the barrister in his thoughts, the Englishman wrote him a letter of thanks. He admitted his thoughts and asked him to tell him how he had saved Giovanni. The barrister wrote him that there were many things in Italy that should not be spoken about. He concluded saying, 'We may meet some day, and then I will tell you what you want to know; not here and now.' But the two men never met.

7 **Giovanni Carlavero was in prison because**

☐ **A.** he was a criminal.

☐ **B.** he had English friends.

☐ **C.** he had fought for Italy's independence.

☐ **D.** he was particularly recommended.

8 **The Englishman decided to talk to Giovanni Carlavero because**

☐ **A.** he was a political prisoner.

☐ **B.** he did not seem to be a real criminal like the other prisoners.

☐ **C.** Charles Dickens had asked him to visit him.

☐ **D.** he was condemned to die.

9 **The Englishman began to visit Giovanni because**

☐ **A.** he found it impossible to stay away from the prison knowing that Giovanni was there suffering.

☐ **B.** he lived in the same town.

☐ **C.** he wanted to discover the reason Giovanni had been condemned.

☐ **D.** he wanted to learn more about Italy's fight for independence.

10 What was strange about the barrister's proposal?

- [ ] **A.** The fact that he wanted so much money.
- [ ] **B.** The fact that he was Italian and wished to help an Englishman.
- [ ] **C.** The fact that he told the Englishman not to ask him any questions about what he was going to do with the money.
- [ ] **D.** The fact that he told the Englishman that he might get Giovanni a pardon with the money.

11 The Englishman finally heard from the Italian barrister about

- [ ] **A.** four months after he gave him one hundred pounds.
- [ ] **B.** six months after he gave him one hundred pounds.
- [ ] **C.** a year and a half after he gave him one hundred pounds.
- [ ] **D.** a year after he gave him one hundred pounds.

12 When the Englishman received the second letter from the Italian barrister he thought that

- [ ] **A.** the barrister was about to have Giovanni freed.
- [ ] **B.** the barrister had already freed Giovanni.
- [ ] **C.** the barrister only wanted to get his money and had not done anything for Giovanni.
- [ ] **D.** he should ask the barrister some questions about what he was really doing.

13 The Englishman changed his mind and sent the barrister fifty pounds because

- [ ] **A.** he was rich and fifty pounds did not matter to him.
- [ ] **B.** the beautiful spring day made him so sad for Giovanni that he decided to take another chance.
- [ ] **C.** the beautiful spring day made him realise that the barrister was probably honest.
- [ ] **D.** he realised that he would never understand certain things about Italy.

14 The Englishman admitted to the Italian barrister that he

- [ ] **A.** knew Giovanni was a political prisoner.

B. thought that the barrister only wanted to trick him out of his money.

C. was very thankful for all that the barrister had done.

D. had seen Giovanni.

Part 3

You are going to read an adaptation of a description by Charles Dickens of four interesting sisters. Five sentences have been removed from the article. Choose from the sentences A-G the one which fits each gap (15-19). There is one extra sentence which you do not need to use. There is an example at the beginning (0).

THE FOUR SISTERS (from *Sketches by Boz*)

This particular street contains more peculiar people than we can describe in this limited space. **0** E Here, then, without any preface, are four of them. The four Miss Willises came to live on our street thirteen years ago, and I must say that even thirteen years ago the Miss Willises were not at all young. When they arrived they painted the house, put the garden in order and brought much fine furniture. **15**

At last, the Miss Willises moved in, and the neighbours began to visit them. The house was the perfection of order, and so were the four Miss Willises. **16** Not a single chair in the whole house was ever seen out of its place, and not a single Miss Willis of the four was ever seen out of hers.

They always sat in the same places doing precisely the same things at the same hour. The eldest Miss Willis used to knit, the second to draw, the others to play duets on the piano. **17** If the eldest Miss Willis became irritable, then all four Miss Willises became irritable immediately. If the oldest Miss Willis became ill-tempered and religious, then all four became ill-tempered and religious directly. Whatever the oldest did, the others did, and whatever anybody else did, they all disapproved of.

Three years went by in this way when an unexpected and extraordinary thing happened: the Miss Willises showed symptoms of summer and their cold life began to warm up. Was it possible? **18** Now where on earth the husband came from, and how the four Miss Willises persuaded themselves that it was possible for a man to marry one of them, without marrying all of them, are questions so difficult to answer.

In any case, it is certain that a man named Mr Robinson came and courted the Miss Willises. **19** [ ] This problem became even more complex when the eldest Miss Willis announced, 'WE are going to marry Mr Robinson.'

A   One of the four Miss Willises was going to be married!

B   Everything was formal, rigid and cold, and so were the four Miss Willises.

C   The neighbours, of course, were anxious to know which of the four sisters he was going to marry.

D   That summer was the hottest I can remember.

E   So, we will only present six of them.

F   They seemed to have no separate existence.

G   So, the neighbours said among themselves that four unmarried women with much money had arrived.

Part 4

You are going to read an adaptation of an extract from Dickens's novel *Great Expectations*. It is about a young boy named Pip. In this scene, Pip's uncle Mr Pumblechook has taken him to the house of a mysterious old lady named Miss Havisham.

For questions 20 to 27 choose from the characters (A-D). There is an example at the beginning (0).

A. Mr Pumblechook   **B. Pip**   **C. Estella**   **D. Miss Havisham**

0	C	Who calls out from the window?
20		Whose feelings are hurt because he/she is not invited in?
21		Who tells Pip to be a good boy?
22		Who takes Pip to Miss Havisham's room?
23		Who lies to Miss Havisham?
24		Who is wearing a wedding dress?
25		Who is proud of his/her emotionally suffering?
26		Who tells Pip to play?

A window was raised, and a clear voice demanded 'What name?' To which my conductor replied, 'Pumblechook.' The window was shut again, and a young lady came across the courtyard, with keys in her hand.

'This,' said Mr Pumblechook, 'is Pip.'

'This is Pip, is it?' returned the girl, who was very pretty and seemed very proud. 'Come in, Pip.'

Mr Pumblechook was coming in also, when she stopped him with the gate.

'Oh!' she said. 'Did you wish to see Miss Havisham?'

'If Miss Havisham wished to see me,' returned Mr Pumblechook very uncomfortably.

'Ah!' said the girl, 'but you see, she doesn't.'

She said it so finally that Mr Pumblechook, even though his dignity was offended, could not protest. But he looked at me severely – as if I had done anything to him! – and left, saying angrily, 'Boy! Let your behaviour here be a credit to your sister!'

This girl, whose name was Estella, led me into the house.

At last we came to the door of a room, and she said, 'Go in.'

I knocked, and was told from within to enter. I entered, therefore, and found myself in a pretty large room, well lighted with wax candles. No glimpse of daylight was to be seen in it. It was a dressing room.

I saw that everything within my view which ought to be white, had been white long ago, and had lost its lustre, and was faded and yellow. I saw that the bride within the bridal dress had dried like the dress, and like the flowers, and had no brightness left but the brightness of her sunken eyes. I saw that the dress had been put upon the rounded figure of a young woman, and that the figure upon which it now hung loose, had shrunk to skin and bone.

'Who is it?' said the lady at the table.

'Pip, ma'am.'

'Come nearer; let me look at you. Come close.'

It was when I stood before her, avoiding her eyes, that I took note of the surrounding objects in detail, and saw that her watch had stopped at twenty minutes to nine, and that a clock in the room had stopped at twenty minutes to nine.

'Look at me,' said Miss Havisham. 'You are not afraid of a woman who has never seen the sun since you were born?'

I am sorry to say that I was not afraid of telling the enormous lie included in the answer 'No.'

'Do you know what I touch here?' she said, laying her hands, one upon the other, on her left side.

'Your heart.'

'Broken!'

She said that word with an eager look, and with strong emphasis, and with a strange smile that had a kind of boast in it.

'I am tired,' said Miss Havisham. 'I want amusement, and I have done with men and women. Play.'

PAPER 2

Writing

1 You live in London and an American friend of yours wants to come to London to see buildings and places important in Dickens's novels. Write her a letter of between 120-180 words in which you suggest that she visit:

- Poet's Corner in Westminster Abbey where Dickens is buried
- Lincoln's Inn, the heart of England's legal system, which was satirised by Dickens
- St Paul's Cathedral, which appears in many novels
- The Dickens's House Museum

Recommend Dickens's House Museum as a good starting point for her Dickens tour. Give her the following information:

- Address – 48 Doughty Street
- Nearest tube stations: Russell Square, Chancery Lane, Holborn
- Hours – Monday – Saturday 10 am to 5 pm
- Sunday 11 am to 5pm
- Admission Charges: Adults £4.00, Students £3.00

Conclude letter by:

- Suggesting she also visit Dickens's seaside home 'Bleakhouse' on the coast of Kent (you are willing to drive her any Sunday).

2 Many modern readers have conflicting feelings about Sydney Carton's sacrifice, especially because Dickens never really tells us why he feels so bad about his life. His only 'crime' seems to be that his job brought him into close contact with many criminals and dishonest people. In 120-180 words say what you think about his sacrifice.

PAPER 3

Use of English

Part 1

For questions 1-15 read the text below and decide which answer A, B, C or D best fits each space. There is an example at the beginning (0).

Example:

        0 A. before   **B.** first   **C.** ago   **D.** ago

NIGHT WALKS (adapted from *The Uncommercial Traveller*)

Some years (**0**).........C......... I had a hard time (**1**).................... asleep and this caused me to walk about the streets of London for a series of (**2**).................... nights.

During those nights I learned much (**3**).................... what it means to live without a house. My principal object was to (**4**).................... through the night, and this activity brought me into sympathetic relations with homeless people (**5**).................... have no other object every night in the year.

The restlessness of a great city, and the (**6**).................... in which it moves around before it can get to sleep, is one of the first entertainments of us homeless people. This period lasted about two hours. We (**7**).................... a great (**8**).................... of company when the public houses closed, but some carriages and people were (**9**).................... with us homeless people. If we were lucky, we saw a policeman, but, in general, there was (**10**).................... little to see.

Finally, though, after the last sellers of pies and hot potatoes went to bed, London fell asleep. Then a homeless person hopes to find any sign of

company, any lighted place, any movement, anything that suggests that
(11).................... else is awake.

Under the light rain I walked to Waterloo-bridge because I was happy to
spend a halfpenny for the chance to say 'Good-night' to the man who
(12).................... the money, and to see for a moment his warm fire. His good
fire and his good great-coat were fine things to see, and he gave me my
change (13).................... a man who was not at all afraid of the night with all
(14).................... sad thoughts, and didn't (15).................... when it became
light again.

1. **A** falling	**B** being	**C** going	**D** coming
2. **A** less	**B** little	**C** few	**D** several
3. **A** of	**B** by	**C** about	**D** around
4. **A** go	**B** be	**C** come	**D** get
5. **A** who	**B** which	**C** than	**D** whom
6. **A** fashion	**B** way	**C** method	**D** mode
7. **A** lose	**B** have lost	**C** lost	**D** had lost
8. **A** a lot	**B** many	**C** deal	**D** much
9. **A** left	**B** stayed	**C** remained	**D** been
10. **A** much	**B** greatly	**C** very	**D** hardly
11. **A** anyone	**B** no one	**C** something	**D** someone
12. **A** collects	**B** gathers	**C** brings	**D** selects
13. **A** as	**B** similar	**C** like	**D** equal
14. **A** its	**B** it's	**C** his	**D** her
15. **A** care	**B** interest	**C** import	**D** worry

Part 2

**For questions 16-30, read the adapted text below and think of the word
which best fits each space. Use only one word in each space. There is an
example at the beginning (0).**

THE CHILD'S STORY

Once upon a (0)..........time.........., a good many years ago, (16).................... was a
traveller, and he set out on a journey. It was a magic journey, and it seemed
very long when he began it, and very short when he had completed half of it.
He travelled (17).................... a rather dark road for some little time, without
meeting anything until at (18).................... he came to a beautiful child. So he
said to the child, 'What do you do here?' And the child said, 'I am always at

163

play. Come and play with me!'

So he played with the child, the whole day long and **(19)**..................... were very merry. The sky was blue, the sun was bright and the water was sparkling. They had plenty of the finest toys **(20)**..................... the world and the most astonishing picture books all **(21)**..................... giants, fairies, bean-stalks, riches, genies, caverns and forests.

But, one day, suddenly, the traveller lost the child. He called to him over and over again, but got no answer. So he went upon his road and went **(22)**..................... for a little while without meeting anything until at last he came to a handsome boy. So, he said to the boy, 'What do you do here?' And the boy said, 'I am always learning. Come and learn with me.'

So he learned with the boy about Jupiter and Juno, and the Greeks and the Romans. But they were not always learning. They had the merriest games that ever **(23)**..................... played. They rowed upon the river in summer, and skated on the ice in **(24)**..................... . Still, one day, in the middle of all these pleasures, the traveller lost the boy, **(25)**..................... he had lost the child, and after calling to him in vain, went on upon his journey. So he went on for a little **(26)**..................... without seeing anything, until at last he came to a young man. So, he said to the young man, 'What do you do here?' And the young man said, 'I am always **(27)**..................... love. Come and love with me.'

So, he went away with that young man, and soon they met one of the prettiest girls that was ever **(28)**..................... . And the young man and the girl always wanted to be together. Sometimes they fought but they always made it up, and they wrote **(29)**..................... other letters every day.

But the traveller lost **(30)**..................... one day, as he lost the rest of his friends, and after a while he came to a middle-aged gentleman. So, he said to the gentleman, 'What are you doing here?' And his answer was, 'I am always busy. Come and be busy with me!'

Part 3

For questions 31-38, use the word given to complete the second sentence so that it has a similar meaning to the first sentence. Do not change the word given. You must use between two and five words, including the word given. There is an example at the beginning (0).

| 0 | It is possible that he will die on the guillotine tomorrow. |

may

He ...._may die on the guillotine_........ tomorrow.

31 'I'm leaving Paris tomorrow,' said Mr Lorry.

was

Mr Lorry said .... the next day.

32 Jacques is the cruellest man in Paris.

than

No one in Paris .... Jacques.

33 Mme Defarge hates Miss Pross, and Miss Pross hates Mme Defarge.

each

Madame Defarge .... other.

34 Even though I am very afraid I must go.

fear

Despite .... go.

35 When he arrived in Paris, he was immediately arrested.

as

He was arrested .... in Paris.

36 He asked Lucy what she was doing in Paris.

are

'Lucy, ... in Paris?' asked Charles.

37 In the past people were executed in France with the guillotine, but not anymore.

used

In France people .... the guillotine.

38 The English had even tried him.

by

He .... the English.

Part 4

For questions 39-54 read the text below and look carefully at each line. Some of the lines are correct and some have a word which should not be there. If a line is correct put a tick (✓) by the number below. If a line has a word which should not be there, write the word by the number. There are two examples at the beginning (0 and 00).

THE THEATRICAL YOUNG GENTLEMAN (from *Sketches by Boz*)

0	The theatrical young gentleman has early and important information
00	have on all theatrical topics. 'Well,' says he, suddenly, when you
39	have meet him in the street, 'this is a problem. The famous actor
40	Flimkins refuses to do a part in the melodrama at the Surrey Theatre.'
41	'And what can there be done?' you ask with as much seriousness as
42	you can pretend. 'Ah, that's the point,' replies the theatrical young
43	gentleman, looking very much serious. 'That other famous actor,
44	Boozle, positively refuses it too. From what I have heard, Boozle
45	would be great in that there role and he would certainly make a great
46	hit in it. But he refuses because they asked to Flimkins to do the role
47	before they asked him, and now nothing on earth could make him do
48	it. 'It's a fine part too. He has to kill six of people during the play and
49	to fight over on a burning bridge, which the public always loves. I
50	have also heard that the last scene, when he is poisoned and then
51	stabbed, will be the greatest thing that anybody has ever done for
52	many years.' After having giving you this piece of news, and placing
53	his finger on his lips to let you to know that it is a big secret, the
54	theatrical young gentleman hurries away.

0. ✔   **00.** have   **39.** ....   **40.** ....   **41.** ....   **42.** ....   **43.** ....   **44.** ....   **45.** ....
46. ....   **47.** ....   **48.** ....   **49.** ....   **50.** ....   **51.** ....   **52.** ....   **53.** ....   **54.** ....

Part 5

For questions 55-64 read the text below. Use the word given in capitals at the end of each line to form a word that fits in the space in the same line. There is an example at the beginning (0).

THOUGHTS ABOUT PEOPLE (from *Sketches by Boz*)

It is strange with how little attention, good, bad, or
(0). indifferent.., a man may live and die in London. He   DIFFERENT
awakens no sympathy in the heart of any single person. His
(55)................. interests no one except himself. You   EXIST
cannot say that he is **(56).................** when he dies because   FORGET
no one remembered him when he was **(57).................** .   LIVE
There is an **(58).................** large group of people in this   INCREDIBLE
great metropolis who do not seem to possess a single

friend, and who nobody appears to care for. (59).................... then forces them to leave their homes in the country and come to London to look for work. It is hard, we know, to break our ties with our homes and friends. It is even (60).................... to cancel the thousand memories of happy days and old times. These men, however, (61).................... for them, have long forgotten such thoughts.

DESPERATE

HARD

FORTUNATE

Old friends in the country have died or (62)....................; people with whom they used to correspond have also become lost in the crowd and (63)...................... of some busy city. Now, these men have become passive creatures of habit and (64)...................... .

MIGRATE

CONFUSE

ENDURE

PAPER 4

Listening Comprehension

Part 1

Listen to this extract from Chapter 2. For questions 1-6, choose the best answers (A, B or C).

1 **What was the man unloading?**
- [ ] **A.** a barrel of wine
- [ ] **B.** large bottles of wine
- [ ] **C.** barrels of wine

2 **How did the people react after they had drunk the wine?**
- [ ] **A.** They became quite sad.
- [ ] **B.** They smiled and laughed.
- [ ] **C.** They shouted and screamed.

3 **What did the man scrawl on the wall?**
- [ ] **A.** a slogan against the king
- [ ] **B.** a slogan against the nobility
- [ ] **C.** the word 'blood'

4 **What was the woman in the wine shop doing?**
- [ ] **A.** knitting
- [ ] **B.** laughing
- [ ] **C.** sewing

5 Who entered the wine shop?

- [ ] **A.** a middle-aged man and a girl
- [ ] **B.** a lady and a gentleman
- [ ] **C.** Madame Defarge and Monsieur Defarge

6 Why was the old man locked in the room?

- [ ] **A.** Because he was a prisoner.
- [ ] **B.** Because he was frightened of strangers.
- [ ] **C.** Because he was frightened of freedom.

Part 2

🎧 **E-2** Listen to this extract from Chapter 3. For questions 7-12 complete the missing information. You will need a word or a short phrase.

The young girl appeared to be	**7**
Charles Darnay was accused of	**8**
John Barsad said that he had stopped being Darnay's friend when he discovered that	**9**
Barsad said that his income came from	**10**
The prosecuting counsel first asked Mr Lorry about when he was	**11**
Mr Lorry said that he had seen the prisoner on	**12**

Part 3

🎧 **E-3** Listen to this extract from Chapter 9. For questions 13-18, identify the correct character (A-D). You can choose a letter more than once.

A. Miss Pross   **B.** Solomon   **C.** Jerry   **D.** Sydney Carton

Who is afraid that people will know who he/she really is?	**13**
Who tells Miss Pross to leave?	**14**
Who tries to remember the name Solomon used in England but can't?	**15**
Who remembers the surname Solomon used in England?	**16**
Who has just arrived in Paris?	**17**
Who is staying with Mr Lorry?	**18**

Part 4

 Listen to this extract from Chapter 5. For questions 19-23 decide whether the statements are true (T) or false (F).

Sydney Carton felt that he could never change his life.   **19** ☐

Sydney Carton had loved Lucie since the first time he saw her.   **20** ☐

Doctor Manette was truly happy that Lucie was getting married.   **21** ☐

Doctor Manette went to see Charles to tell him his real name.   **22** ☐

Doctor Manette did not feel well after talking with Charles.   **23** ☐

PAPER 5

Speaking

Part 1

Ask and answer questions with your partner to find out about each other (name, age, leisure activities); and your families (names and what they do), friends (their names, ages and why you like them), school life (best and worst subjects, favourite teacher) and plans for the future.

Part 2

Look at the picture on pages 60 and 61. Pretend that you were a member of the crowd and that your partner was one of the soldiers defending the Bastille. Say how you both felt during this historic moment. Then change roles.

Part 3

With your partner decide which famous actors and actress you would have in the roles of Charles Darnay, Sydney Carton and Lucie Manette. Make sure that you are able to explain why they would be good for the roles.

Part 4

Now discuss which parts of the story should be developed and emphasised the most in a modern film version of *A Tale of Two Cities*. The political side? The violence? The love story? The sacrifice of Sydney Carton? Others?

A Tale of Two Cities

KEY TO THE ACTIVITIES, EXIT TEST AND FCE EXIT TEST

CHARLES DICKENS

Page 11   Exercise 1

a. His father was imprisoned for debt.
b. He had to go to work in a factory.
c. The theme of poor or abandoned children.
d. *The Pickwick Papers.*
e. *Oliver Twist* and *Nicholas Nickleby.*
f. Because of the high quality of his writing.

Chapter One

Page 12   Exercise 1

1. A   2. C   3. B   4. C
5. C   6. C   7. C   8. A

Page 20   Exercise 1

a. Jerry, a messenger from Tellson's Bank.
b. 'Recalled to life.'
c. Because he had been thinking about sad and painful events of the past.
d. She was a slender girl of about seventeen with golden hair.
e. She knew that her father had been French and had lived in Beauvais and that he had married an English lady.
f. Because she had guessed that Mr Lorry was about to tell her that her father wasn't dead after all.
g. She learned that her father had not died but had been put in prison by powerful enemies, and that now he was in Paris.
h. She thought that he had unnecessarily traumatised Miss Manette by not using more tact in telling her about her father.

Page 20   Exercise 2

a. In the beginning he pretended that he was not talking about her father, and so Miss Manette had to guess the meaning of what Mr Lorry was saying. In other words, his way of telling the story built up the tension too much.
b. He let the reader guess the true meaning of his story without explaining everything first.
c. Open answer.
d. He feels that he has to act as a professional, even in this very

painful and emotional situation. Still, it is obvious from his loss of sleep and his obsessive repeating that it was not just a matter of business, that he felt very emotionally involved.

e. Dickens does not tell us the purpose of Lorry's journey to Dover at first. Also he does not tell us the meaning of the message, 'Recalled to Life' until the end. Finally, we, like Miss Manette, are kept in suspense by the storytelling of Mr Lorry.

Page 21   Exercise 3

1. Definition ii. The use is oddly poetic because Mr Lorry is using the word in its official sense, but the person is called back from Death.

2. **a.** iii   **b.** ii   **c.** i
   d. i   **e.** iii   **f.** ii

Page 22   Exercise 4

Sample letter

The biggest shock I ever had in my life was when I received a letter from Mr Lorry telling me to meet him in Dover. I assumed he wanted to tell me about my father's property.

Now, I knew that I had been brought to England from France after my parents' death when I was a little girl. You can imagine how I felt when Mr Lorry started telling me about a child with a French father and an English mother, everybody thought the father was dead but he was in fact still alive. It seemed impossible, and I suppose it would have been better if he had told me the news plainly or if he had written a letter. As it was, the shock was too great and I fainted.

Later I realised that Mr Lorry could think of no way of telling me about my father other than in his oddly official way and that he was as overwhelmed as I was. So, in the end, I forgave Mr Lorry for having given me such a shock.

Chapter Two

Page 22   Exercise 1

a. L   **b.** D   **c.** D   **d.** L
e. L   **f.** O   **g.** M

Page 28   Exercise 1

a. F – They were mostly poor and ill-fed.

b. F – People rushed up to get some of the wine to drink for themselves.

c. T

d. T

e. T

f. T

g. T

h. T

i. T

j. F – They are going to live in London.

Page 28   Exercise 2

1. He thinks that she is his dead wife.

2. Because she resembles his dead wife so much, and he has never seen his daughter as a young woman.

Page 29   Exercise 3

The scene shows how the poor people's anger would eventually explode because of some casual incident such as the breaking of a barrel of wine. The wine symbolises all the blood that would flow during the French Revolution and its immediate aftermath. Finally, the drunkenness from the wine anticipates the drunkenness from violence which would later occur.

Sample answer to filming the scene

- Tracking shot along the street, showing the poor people and the general dirtiness. (20 seconds)
- Long shot of man with cart and barrel of wine. (5 seconds)
- Tracking shot moving towards the man with the cart. (5 seconds)
- Close-up of the upsetting of the barrel. (20 seconds)
- Panning shot, intermixed with close-ups of people on the streets, showing the reactions of the people as they realise what is happening. (20 seconds)
- Series of close-ups of different people scooping up the wine and dirtying their faces. (30 seconds)
- Close-up of the man who decides to write on wall as he dips his finger in wine. (10 seconds)
- Panning shot, intermixed with close-ups, showing the reactions of the people in the crowd to the word 'blood'. (30 seconds)
- Panning shot that finds M. Defarge, and fixes on him for a close-up, showing his frowning disapproval. (15 seconds)
- Panning shot passing from close-up of M. Defarge to Madame Defarge's disapproving face, moving down to a close-up of her knitting fingers. (15 seconds)
- Close-up of knitting fingers

alternating with close-ups of the drunken, wine-stained faces of the crowd. (20 seconds)

Chapter Three

Page 30   Exercise 1

1. ✓   2. ✓   3. on   4. ✓   5. had
6. ✓   7. himself   8. to   9. ✓
10. to   11. ✓   12. is / 's
13. have   14. ✓   15. ✓   16. up
17. into   18. for   19. ✓

Page 37   Exercise 1

1. B   2. C   3. C   4. A
5. C   6. A   7. B   8. D

Page 38   Exercise 2

a. He implies that he has always had problems with money, and that he is really accusing Charles Darnay because he does not want to pay back the money he owes him.

b. He does not use quotation marks and he does not use expressions such as 'he asked', 'he answered' and so on.

c. Here Dickens omits all the expressions such as 'he asked', 'he replied' and so on.

d. It lets us imagine the quickness of the questions and answers between counsel and the witness.

e. They switch rapidly from a close-up of the face of the counsel that is questioning to a close-up of the witness, and back again.

Page 39   Exercise 3

The title of the novel itself shows us that Dickens wanted to talk about both Paris and London. He also wanted to present the parallels between the barbarities of the French Revolution, and the cruelties of the British legal system, both with regard to its form of punishment and its cruel slowness, which he dissects and satirises in other books such as *Bleak House*.

Chapter Four

Page 46   Exercise 1

1. H   **2.** B   **3.** I   **4.** G   **5.** C
6. J   **7.** D   **8.** A   **9.** E
F not used

Page 46   Exercise 2

a. He shows how the making of a simple cup of hot chocolate had been turned into a Gargantuan enterprise requiring the efforts of four men, and all this is to satisfy the silly ego of Monseigneur.

b. The Marquis is disgusted simply because the sight and smell of poverty offends his refined senses. Dickens, too, is offended by the horrible things he saw and smelled, but he is also offended that some human beings force other human beings to live in such horrible conditions.

Page 47   Exercise 3

Paragraph order
a. 5   **b.** 4   **c.** 2   **d.** 1
e. 7   **f.** 3   **g.** 8   **h.** 6

Cloze answers
1. health   **2.** evidence   **3.** treason
4. spy   **5.** wine shop   **6.** shoes
7. wife   **8.** England   **9.** mail
10. mademoiselle   **11.** mist
12. blunderbuss   **13.** highwaymen

14. Recalled   **15.** chateau
16. Marquis   **17.** father   **18.** tremble
19. faint   **20.** give   **21.** rotten
22. dagger   **23.** drive
24. condemned   **25.** certain
26. acquitted

Chapter Five

Page 49-50   Exercise 1

1. in   **2.** on   **3.** was   **4.** there
5. did   **6.** whose   **7.** him   **8.** his
9. be   **10.** who   **11.** For   **12.** can
13. of   **14.** later   **15.** done

Page 55   Exercise 1

a. He was a French teacher.
b. He was an intelligent man who was often sad and bitter.
c. He became frightened.
d. Because he loved Lucie but he felt that he lived a bad life and could never change.
e. Anything to help her or the ones she loved, and at any cost.
f. He went pale and started trembling.

Page 55   Exercise 2

1. He realises that he can never marry Lucie because, in his opinion, he has led a bad life, but he says he will do anything to help her or the ones she loves. Of course, he realises that among the ones she loves is Charles Darnay whom he does not like.

2. *Sample letter*
   I fell in love with Lucie Manette the first time I saw her in the Old Bailey. My colleague and I were

defending a certain Charles Darnay, who was accused of treason. Lucie was there and was very concerned for Mr Darnay. Her beauty struck me but I was not happy that she worried so much about Mr Darnay, whom I found a bit pompous and affected.

Now Lucie is marrying that intolerable man and although I do not think him worthy, I sadly cannot allow myself to ask her to be mine. My life has been infected by the squalor of criminal life that I deal with every day and I must not bring her into contact with the dark world that is mine. After I had told her, I felt horrible, but then I was content at least that I had not brought such a lovely, angelic creature into ruin.

Even if I am unworthy of Lucie, I hope that my love for her will some day help her to lead a happy life.

Chapter Six

Page 56-57   Exercise 1

1. went   2. Mr Lorry
3. Sydney Carton   4. wine   5. night
6. customers   7. valuables   8. soon
9. news   10. Paris   11. Defarge
12. Bastille   13. Swords   14. sea
15. happening

Page 64   Exercise 1

a.   F – After their marriage he no longer suffered from his illness.
b.   F – He came to visit them every Sunday.
c.   F – He was careful not to drink wine on the days of his visits.
d.   T
e.   F – The women attacked as well.
f.   T

g.   F – He found some papers.
h.   T
i.   F – He gave him the letter because Charles Darnay said to him that he knew the Marquis St Evrémonde and could deliver the letter.
j.   T
k.   F – He did leave Lucie.
l.   F – Charles went to France to help Gabelle, and Mr Lorry went there for the bank's customers.

Page 65   Exercise 2

1. e.   It was dangerous to travel to France because the revolution had begun there.
2. l.   Miss Manette recognised Mr Darnay at the trial because she had seen him on the boat returning from France.
3. a.   Charles decided to travel to Paris because his servant Gabelle had written him a letter.
4. g.   Doctor Manette looked pale because Charles had told him his real name.
5. i.   Mr Lorry waited at Dover because he received a message from his bank.
6. c.   The Marquis de Evrémonde was not able to obtain a *lettre de cachet* because he had fallen out of favour with the court.
7. d.   Mr Lorry brought Lucie to England because her father had disappeared.
8. f.   There was a lot of excitement around the castle because someone had killed the Marquis.
9. k.   Jacques cried because the Marquis had killed his child.
10. h.   There were the initials A.M. on the wall because it had been Doctor Manette's cell.

11. b. Charles gave up the Evrémonde title because his family had done many cruel things.

12. j Miss Manette fainted because she had thought her father was dead.

Page 67   Exercise 3

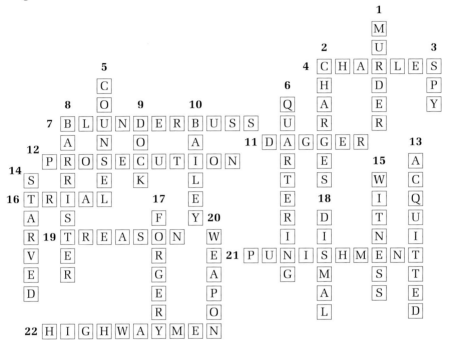

THE FRENCH REVOLUTION

Page 72   Exercise 1

a. The clergy and the nobility.

b. It was divided into three large groups known as 'estates': the clergy, the nobility and the bourgeoisie.

c. They had been sent to help Washington's army.

d. The right to take up arms against a tyranny; no taxation without representation; and the rights of man.

e. It was a meeting of representatives of the three estates of France, which was summoned by Louis XVI.

f. To face the discontent of the bourgeoisie that wanted a greater role in the government, and that of the nobles and clergy who feared that they would have to start paying taxes.

g. The government formed by the Third Estate after they had declared that they were the real representatives of France.

h. The Bastille, a prison, was attacked and taken by an angry crowd.

i. It abolished tax exemptions and issued the Rights of Man.

j. Because the monarchies of Austria and Prussia tried to restore the old monarchy in France.

k. In January, 1793.

l. A period of extreme violence when thousands of people were killed on the guillotine.

Chapter Seven

Page 73   Exercise 1

1. A   **2.** C   **3.** C   **4.** C   **5.** B   **6.** A

Page 77   Exercise 1

a. check his papers.

b. arrested and thrown into prison.

c. Charles had been arrested.

d. been murdered by the crowd.

e. the guillotine.

f. he had been a prisoner in the Bastille for eighteen years.

g. carry people to the guillotine.

h. he did not want them to know that he was in Paris just yet.

Page 77   Exercise 2

a. treated him

b. found out (that) he was

c. as soon as he arrived

d. they had to save

e. Doctor Manette what he was doing

f. they would free

g. the doctor to see

Page 78   Exercise 3

1. C   **2.** A   **3.** B   **4.** C   **5.** A

Chapter Eight

Page 86   Exercise 1

a. Because that was his noble name before he renounced it.

b. At first they are quite hostile, but after they hear the testimony of Gabelle and Doctor Manette, they are on his side.

c. He testifies in his favour, confirming what Darnay had said about his title and the family property.

d. Because Lucie is the daughter of Doctor Manette, who is a kind of hero of the Revolution.

e. He tells the court that Charles had been tried for treason by the English.

f. They find him not guilty.

g. Because he was responsible for getting Charles acquitted.

h. Monsieur and Madame Defarge, and another unknown person.

Page 86   Exercise 2

Fickle fits the behaviour of the courtroom crowd perfectly because they first jeer Darnay and then when he is acquitted they treat him as a kind of hero.

Page 87   Exercise 3

a. was driving

b. had been dancing

c. had been working

d. were arguing

e. had been swimming

f. had been playing

g. were playing

h. had been smoking

Page 88 Exercise 4

1. F **2.** D **3.** A **4.** B
C & E not used

Chapter Nine

Page 91 Exercise 1

1. C **2.** D **3.** A **4.** B **5.** A
6. C **7.** D **8.** D **9.** A **10.** B
11. A **12.** D **13.** C **14.** B **15.** A

Page 99 Exercise 1

a. F – She went there to do some shopping.
b. T
c. T
d. T
e. F – He knew quite well that he was a spy in the French prisons.
f. T
g. T
h. F – He himself is the informer in the French prison that Sydney Carton refers to.
i. F – He agrees because Sydney Carton will tell the authorities that he was once a spy for the English government if he doesn't help.
j. F – Sydney Carton says that he is not talking about helping Charles Darnay escape.

Page 99 Exercise 2

● We can consider this a coincidence because Mr Lorry would later receive the letter from Gabelle addressed to Charles. Then as we will soon learn Charles's family was responsible for the imprisonment of Doctor Manette, one of Mr Lorry's customers.

● Miss Pross was Lucie's nurse, and it certainly is a coincidence that the man who testified against Charles Darnay and who is later in a position to help him escape from the French prison, is Lucie's nurse's brother.

Page 100 Exercise 3

Sample answer

I realise that nowadays my friends are used to seeing films with incredible special effects and amazing colours, but I think this black and white film from 1935 will surprise them, as out of the seven versions made since 1911 it is unanimously considered the best.

The main reason I think my friends would enjoy this film is because the acting is so good and the films we most appreciate have both great acting and a great story. Well, the story we already know is great, and the actors in this film are considered by critics, then and now, as some of the best that ever worked for Hollywood. Indeed, Ronald Colman as Sydney Carton is a classic. The same is true of the minor roles. Basil Rathbone, later famous for his role as Sherlock Holmes, gives a great performance as the evil Marquis Evrémonde.

Finally, I think my friends will be surprised how beautiful and effective black and white photography can be.

Chapter Ten

Page 101 Exercise 1

Open answer.

Page 110   Exercise 1

1. B   **2.** C   **3.** A   **4.** C   **5.** D
6. A   **7.** B   **8.** C   **9.** B   **10.** C

Page 112   Exercise 2

a.   The great hatred of Madame
       Defarge derives from the great evil
       done to her family, and now she
       wishes to do evil to the
       Evrémonde family in return.

b.   Love. Doctor Manette's love for
       his daughter allows him to
       overcome the hate he feels for the
       Evrémonde family, at least as far
       as Charles is concerned.

Page 113   Exercise 3

Sample answer

    In the novel *A Tale of Two Cities*
Charles Dickens does not present
Madame Defarge as a victim, as would
be expected, but as the villain. The
death of her brother, sister, brother-in-
law and indirectly her father, all at the
hands of Charles's father, the Marquis
Evrémonde and his twin brother, has
incensed in her an anger and a
somewhat understandable desperate
desire for revenge. Now her extension
of that vengeful desire also includes
Lucie, Doctor Manette and Charles,
who are not even remotely connected
with the evil her family suffered,
causes us to lose our sympathy with
her.

    Had I written this novel, I would
have presented a more complete
portrait of this desperate woman,
while keeping all the darkness and
hatred of her character. I would have
brought out that her evil actions are
really a continuation of the suffering
she must have felt when her family all
died at the hands of those two
aristocratic brothers; and that her
constant search for bloody revenge
means that she has not yet left the hell
of some twenty years earlier.

Chapter Eleven

Page 114   Exercise 1

1. day   **2.** thought   **3.** die   **4.** letter
5. nothing   **6.** uncle   **7.** told
8. daughter   **9.** responsible
10. finished   **11.** woke   **12.** began
13. guillotine   **14.** like   **15.** struck

Page 121   Exercise 1

a.   That he had known nothing about
       all the horrible things his father
       and uncle had done.

b.   That he did not consider him
       responsible in any way for his
       death, even if he was the witness
       who had made the court condemn
       him to death.

c.   That he too was a prisoner.

d.   Because he does not ask him to
       escape, but has him carried out of
       the prison after he has been
       drugged to sleep. Finally, a
       'Charles Darnay' does go to the
       guillotine.

e.   He asks him to change boots and
       cravat with him, and to write a
       note to Lucie.

f.   He is referring to the time when
       he promised Lucie that he would
       do anything at all to help her or
       her loved ones.

g.   He is carried out of the prison
       unconscious.

h.   The seamstress.

Page 122   Exercise 2 A

a. He heard the crowd yell.

b. He heard the dog barking under his window.

c. I felt something moving in my hair.

d. She felt the rain splashing against her face.

e. He heard the wind whistling through the trees.

f. They saw the robber jump out of the window.

g. The lawyer heard the judge call for silence in the courtroom.

h. We saw the children running up and down the stairs.

Page 123   Exercise 2 B

a. writing

b. fall down

c. sing

d. break, watching, looking

e. flowing

f. burning, shout

g. playing, practising

h. bump

Chapter Twelve

Page 132   Exercise 1

1. H   2. D   3. C   4. I
5. A   6. G   7. F   8. B
E   not used

Page 132   Exercise 2

A. He points out to us that they could not understand each other's language but that by means of their gestures and the tone of their voices they understood each other perfectly. There is something nearly surreal about these two women threatening each other in languages the other can't understand.

B. She becomes deaf as a result of her battle, and her deafness is so complete she cannot hear the dreadful sound of the tumbrils, a sound that has become symbolic for the horrors of the Revolution.

Page 133   Exercise 3 A

a. I'd prefer to eat at home tonight.

b. I'd rather go to the cinema.

c. I'd rather read a mystery story.

d. I'd prefer to talk about it another time.

e. I'd rather not do it.

f. I'd prefer to go home.

Page 134   Exercise 3 B

a. **defend** / we'd rather Sydney Carton defended you.

b. **take** / I'd rather Mr Cruncher took it.

c. **knit** / I'd rather Madame Defarge knitted it.

d. **teach** / I'd rather Charles Darnay taught you.

e. **do** / I'd rather Miss Pross did it.

f. **torture** / we'd rather the Marquis St Evrémonde tortured them.

g. **keep** / I'd rather Mr Lorry kept them.

h. **show** / I'd rather Monsieur Defarge showed you.

i. **examine** / I'd rather Doctor Manette examined her.

HOW DICKENS INTERPRETED THE FRENCH REVOLUTION

Page 137   Exercise 1

a. Charles Dickens did not discuss the politics or the ideologies of the period.
b. He mostly presented how individuals were affected by the French Revolution.
c. He presents them as cruel and corrupt.
d. The story of how Doctor Manette and Madame Defarge's family suffered at the hands of the Evrémondes illustrates these points.
e. When he recounts the storming of the Bastille.
f. The violence of the revolutionaries and their pitiless execution of thousands of people with the guillotine.

Chapter Thirteen

Page 138-139   Exercise 1

1. unhappy   2. prisoners
3. miserable   4. suffering
5. famous   6. intensity
7. anxiously   8. loudly
9. frightened   10. quietly
11. contemptuously   12. recognised
13. execution

Page 144   Exercise 1

a. F – He was singing and dancing because he had gone mad from his suffering.
b. F – He didn't want anybody to realise that Charles Darnay was not there.
c. T
d. T
e. F – He hopes that they will lead happy lives.
f. T

Page 144   Exercise 2

Paragraphs
1. f.   2. b.   3. a.   4. c.   5. g.
6. e.   7. i.   8. h.   9. d.

1. spy   2. traitor   3. beaten
4. escape   5. studying   6. Barsad
7. Pross   8. accuser   9. son-in-law
10. cell   11. taken   12. account
13. descendants   14. wipe
15. Paris   16. dismay   17. brother
18. death   19. Charles   20. tumbril
21. kiss   22. drew   23. crash

Page 146   Exercise 3

1 J E E R I N G
2 B O N N E T
3 S H A M E
4 B E A T E N
5 T U M B R I L S
6 U T T E R
7 C R A V A T
8 D I S M A Y
9 A C C O U N T
10 O U T R A G E O U S

1

1. C   **2.** A   **3.** B   **4.** A   **5.** C
6. D   **7.** B   **8.** D   **9.** A   **10.** A
11. C   **12.** C   **13.** C   **14.** C

2

a. Mr Lorry is referring to his relationship to Doctor Manette and his family, who were indeed his bank's customers, but their relationship was deeply human. He brought Lucie to England after the disappearance of her father, and he brought Lucie the news that her father was alive. Still, Mr Lorry felt the need as an employee of Tellson's Bank to hide the fact that he was working to help Doctor Manette and his daughter because they were, quite simply, his friends.

b. Because 'escape' means that a person tries to get away from prison, while Charles never tries to run away from the prison and would never have accepted to have Sydney died in his place. So, in the end, Charles is carried out of prison, and does not escape.

c. Jacques is referring to the fact that the Marquis' carriage was travelling fast when it killed his daughter, and therefore he wants a carriage to take the dead body of the Marquis quickly to his grave.

3

a. Both the French and English authorities are not honest in the evidence they use against him. In England the authorities use an informer who is obviously not very honest; and in France the authorities use the accusation of a man who would not have willingly accused his own son-in-law.

b. Both punishments, quartering and death by the guillotine, are shown to be barbarous. In addition, both punishments were carried out publicly.

4

a. Both of them suffered greatly at the hands of the Marquis Evrémonde and his twin brother.

b. They are both 'stained' by the world they live in: Charles is stained by the bad actions of his family, and Sydney is stained by the corruption of the English courts.
Both of them try to wipe away this stain: Charles by renouncing his family name and property, and by helping Gabelle; Sydney by dying for Lucie and her family.
They both love Lucie.
Finally, they look alike, which emphasises the fact that they have much in common.

5

a. He accepts her marriage to the son of the man who had him put in prison.

b. He gives up his property and name; and he also comes to France, risking his life, to help a servant of his family.

c. She sacrifices her hearing to save Lucie and her family.

6

a. It shows the drunken violence that will characterise the aftermath of the Revolution.

b. It symbolises the arrogant and absurd waste of the French aristocracy.

c. This shows the momentous nature of her battle with the evil Madame Defarge.

PAPER 1 – Reading Comprehension

Part 1

1. B 2. H 3. E 4. F 5. C 6. A
G not used

Part 2

7. C 8. B 9. A 10. C 11. D
12. C 13. B 14. B

Part 3

15. G 16. B 17. F 18. A 19. C
D not used

Part 4

20. A 21. A 22. C 23. B
24. D 25. D 26. D 27. D

PAPER 2 – Writing

1. *Sample answer*

Dear Susan,

I am so glad you are coming to London, where you will discover many buildings and places connected with Dickens' novels. First, I think you should go to the Dickens' House Museum, which is a great starting point for your explorations. The address is 48 Doughty Street, and you can easily reach it from several tube stations.

After this you might want to go to Westminster Abbey where you can see Dickens' tomb in Poet's Corner. Then, of course, you will want to see Lincoln's Inn, the heart of England's legal system, which was often satirised in his writings. Then you can go to see the fabulous St Paul's Cathedral, which often appears in Dickens' novels and which is worth seeing.

Finally, to escape London, you can go to see Dickens' beautiful seaside home, 'Bleakhouse' on the Kent coast. That too is a lovely place to visit and I would be more than happy to drive you there any Sunday.

Well, that's about all. Can't wait to see you.

Jeremy

2. *Sample answer*

From a personal point of view, I must say that I would not sacrifice myself for such a reason. I do not think that somebody is guilty or bad just because he works with bad people. It is more important what that person does, and if Sydney Carton did not do bad things than I do not see him as a bad person.

Still, from a psychological point of view I can understand him. After all, the corruption and violence at the time was great. Justice was slow and benefited the wealthy as Dickens often showed. So, since Carton had to enter into this system to do his job well, and was immersed in this corrupt world every day, it is understandable that he would feel corrupted and bad too.

Also, since Carton drank, this probably made him feel even worse about himself in the end.

So, the chance to do something truly noble for a woman he idealised probably attracted him greatly, and might have seemed like a kind of liberation from the barbarous world of the courts.

PAPER 3 – Use of English

Part 1

1. A   2. D   3. C   4. D   5. A
6. B   7. C   8. C   9. A   10. C
11. D   12. A   13. C   14. A   15. A

Part 2

16. there   17. along   18. last
19. they   20. in   21. about
22. on   23. were   24. winter
25. as   26. while   27. in
28. seen   29. each   30. him

Part 3

31.   (that) he was leaving Paris
32.   is crueller than
33.   and Miss Pross hate each
34.   my fear, I must
35.   as soon as he arrived
36.   what are you doing
37.   used to be executed with
38.   had even been tried by

Part 4

39. have   40. ✓   41. there   42. ✓
43. much   44. ✓   45. there
46. to (to Flimkins)   47. ✓   48. of
49. over   50. ✓   51. ✓   52. having
53. to (to know)   54. ✓

Part 5

55. existence   56. forgotten
57. alive   58. incredibly
59. Desperation   60. harder
61. fortunately   62. migrated
63. confusion   64. endurance

PAPER 4 - Listening Comprehension

Part 1

1. A   2. B   3. C   4. A   5. A   6. C

Part 2

7.   worried and nervous
8.   treason
9.   he was a spy
10.   property
11.   on the Dover mail
12.   the boat when he returned from France

Part 3

13. B   14. B   15. C
16. D   17. D   18. D

Part 4

19. T   20. T   21. F   22. F   23. T

PAPER 5 – Speaking
Open answers.

Black Cat English Readers